4/12

The
Star
Shard

The Star Shard

by Frederic S. Durbin

Houghton Mifflin
HOUGHTON MIFFLIN HARCOURT
Boston New York 2012

"The Star Shard" was first published in a shorter form as a serial in
Cricket magazine, April 2008–April 2009 issues.

Houghton Mifflin is an imprint of Houghton Mifflin
Harcourt Publishing Company.

www.hmhbooks.com

The text of this book is set in Horley Old Style MT.

Library of Congress Cataloging-in-Publication Data

Durbin, Frederic S., 1966–
The star shard / by Frederic S. Durbin.
p. cm.
Summary: A twelve-year-old slave on a gigantic,
traveling "wagon city" joins forces with a new—and
magical—slave, and as they plan their escape they
encounter mystery, enchantment, and deadly monsters
while their one chance for freedom draws ever nearer.

ISBN 978-0-547-37025-5
[1. Fantasy. 2. Slavery—Fiction. 3. Fairies—Fiction.] I. Title.
PZ7.D93229St 2012
[Fic]—dc23
2011012164

Manufactured in the United States of America
DOC 10 9 8 7 6 5 4 3 2 1
4500339669

For my parents

Chapter 1

Moonpine Blue

To say that the Thunder Rake was a wagon would be to call the sea a puddle, for the Rake was a fortified city, full of workshops and stables, houses, towers, gardens—even a rippling canal. But it also had wheels rimmed with steel, each one seven times as tall as a man, and it had arms made of gigantic tree trunks that slid back and forth, three along each side. Metal claws on the ends crashed down and sank into the earth each time an arm came forward. Like a gargantuan living creature, the Thunder Rake crawled over hills and through valleys. The folk of towns and cities could hear the Rake coming, with its axles squeaking, with rumbles and booms, claw after claw. People flung open wide their gates and flocked out to buy exotic cloth, spices, glass, tools, and hundreds of other goods from the moving city's merchants. All the world was a market, said Rombol, Master of the Rake. Everything could be had for a price.

Between selling journeys, when the merchants had finished their daily stockpiling and inventorying of goods, Cymbril's evening duty was to sing as they gobbled the fine fare of the Rake's main dining hall. Whether they listened or shouted over her voice with their bawdy jokes, her task was to sing.

Her voice filled the hall, drifting out through the narrow windows under the rafters. In her thoughts, she floated away with the notes, riding the warm breeze over forests and fields; but in reality, she could go nowhere. The huge wooden doors of the Rake were shut with her inside. *I'm a slave,* Cymbril reminded herself at times. *I'm kept here just like the birds and the hounds in their cages.* But at least she was warm and dry, clothed and fed, which was more than beggars had. She had watched them in many a town—thin, unwashed folk huddled in rags, pleading for scraps at the end of a market day, when the cooks dumped the dregs from soup kettles and threw bones to the dogs. Cymbril knew some people had much harder lives than her own. Though long workdays were exhausting, she loved to sing.

When the snow was gone and green shoots sprouted in the fields beyond the windows, the wagon-city awoke from its winter slumber. Carpenters hammered on the rooftops, replacing lost shingles, and the mighty wagon trundled down to the ocean.

It was the time of loading. Great ships crowded the harbor at Whaleroad, where the land fell in shelves of grass and rock to the sea. Wagons clattered up and down the streets all day, bringing bundles and barrels to the Rake, rolling away empty. Merchants haggled on every deck with traders from far-off places. Cymbril stood at a window hatch as Master Rombol's people stalked along the wharves, talking with seamen in golden coats and crimson turbans. Some sailors had boots with curling, pointed toes, and curved daggers through their belts. Others had angular eyes, braided beards, or skin the color of bronze. The Rake's folk marked in heavy ledger books as they negotiated, and the traders answered back with flourishing gestures and fingers indicating numbers. Sea captains would turn away, piqued at low offers for their wares; the Rake merchants would call them back, running a few steps to overtake them. All across the piers and up the streets, it was a dance in brilliant colors. Cymbril gazed down with her chin in her palms as the sky deepened to purple. Lanterns began to flicker in the bazaars and on the ships. Smoke billowed from cooking stalls, and the air smelled of spices. Someone unseen plucked a stringed instrument, the melody rising and sinking like ocean swells.

Cymbril squinted across the dark water to the nearest ships, softly creaking under webs of rigging that climbed to the stars. She imagined a girl just like herself hidden somewhere on each one of them, peering out from some tiny hatchway among all the ropes and ladders—a harbor full of girls on ships, all bound for different ports, for different lives far away. Cymbril waved a hand, knowing it was foolish, but always hoping one of the unseen maidens was waving back.

With a sigh, she tipped her face up to the stars, so blazingly bright. A breeze riffled her hair. *Where am I going?* she wondered. *Does life lead anywhere—or only around and around, from town to city to town, and back here in another year to start all over again?*

The hubbub of loading days went on well into the night. Lines of workers passed bales while merchants shouted and argued. Cymbril yearned to explore the seaport, but she was never allowed off the Rake at Whaleroad. Still, it was easy enough to become lost in the chaos aboard and take up her pastime of wandering the endless pathways of Rombol's city. Strictly speaking, her skulk-abouts were not allowed—but as long as she wasn't poking into salable goods, the reproof was typically a gruff "Get to bed!"

Corridors on the Rake had names, like streets: Anvil, Longwander, Tinley, Inbrace, Barrel Corner . . . Cymbril took Ferny Way and ducked beneath a grape arbor. If she stayed out of sight, she could probably get through the evening without having to stock a storeroom or haul parcels into a hold.

Putting up the hood of her cloak, she huddled back into the shadows as a wagon rumbled past, drawn by four horses, down a wooden street inside the Rake. This was Grandway, the major bow-to-stern thoroughfare, with shaded lanterns glowing on its pillars. Three stories high it rose in some stretches, its vault crisscrossed by bridges, its balconies a whirl of activity. She pattered swiftly across the avenue, watching for traffic, and darted toward Fender Lane.

In a track like an alcove with no top, a crank basket hung on its chain. She unfastened the gate and stepped into the basket's round interior. The woven walls were about as high as her elbows. She glanced up at the chain leading away into darkness. The shaft smelled of oil and dust. After rolling her sleeves to keep them well clear of the gears, Cymbril turned the crank. The pulleys were well maintained, like most of the Rake's mechanisms. It took no strength at all to make the basket ascend with a whirring of metal teeth and sprockets. The basket trundled up to the next level and the next. She glided past a fat spider in a web, past an abandoned bird's nest in a triangular junction of beams. Slowing, she stooped to peer into dim crawlspaces between the floors. The Rake had no shortage of mysterious passages, each one begging to be plumbed.

Some people said the colossal wagon had five stories, some said nine, and some said thirteen, for several of the decks were hidden within the walls or couched in balcony half-levels. Despite her explorations, Cymbril had not found a way into three of the inner galleries—yet.

No one waited to use the basket on any of the floors she passed, which suited Cymbril fine. A slave in a crank basket would surely have to explain herself. When she bumped to a stop at the shaft's top, she hopped out into a side portico of Clerestory. She watched and listened.

On the right, the doorway of a teabunk stood open. Inside, the Rake's richest folk sipped from gleaming cups, smoked delicate silver pipes, and lounged on couches. The many-paned windows gazed out across the wide lands, offering spectacular views from the summit of this city that moved. Cymbril knew, for she'd sung in the teabunks, too, in clouds of perfumed vapor. "The King fancies he owns all this," she'd heard Rombol say, pointing out through the leaded glass in a gesture that took in mountains and meadows, castles and towns. "But it belongs to *us*." And all those present had laughed with their Master, Rombol the Magnificent—all but Cymbril, whose task was to sing.

Anything could be had for a price, and the mighty Rake could provide it all: in the merchants' minds, they could sell icicles to the Queen of Winter, the moon's dancing reflection to the sea.

Two giggling women drifted from the open doorway, one fanning herself with a painted fan. They turned in Cymbril's direction with a rustle of silks. The worst sort to meet—tipsy and with the leisure to take note of her, they would see her golden hair, her shining eyes in the gloom of her hood, and they would recognize her—the high ladies of the Rake always did, and they seemed to hate her with one accord. They would not give Cymbril boxes to stack or bundles to carry; rather, they would drag her with their cats' claws into the den of heat and perfume. They would smile sweetly and demand a song she did not know—or knew imperfectly—and they would smirk and cluck their cruelties, taking care to remind her that she would never own so much as a single patch on the oldest threadbare dress in her trunk.

No, these were not the sort to meet, and Cymbril regretted coming anywhere near the teabunks. To avoid the pair, she wriggled into the nearest gap in the wall, a space so narrow she had to edge in sideways. Only the faintest reflection of the hallway's lamp light found its way here. Under her leather slippers, the tiled floor sloped toward the Rake's outer wall. There was a stench of rotten food—she was standing in a channel for slop water. The kitchens on both sides of her had hatches for dumping out bucketfuls of a greasy, soapy tide. Though the footing was dry, she might be wading at any moment. The women were about to pass the mouth of the space. Cymbril moved deeper into the dark, her skirt snagging on a nail head, her hand breaking through cobwebs. Something tickly crawled across her face. Clamping her lips to suppress a whimper, she reached down to touch the reassuring hardness in her pocket. If she needed light, she could have it.

The ladies lingered, their shadows blocking the light. Cymbril's toes found the grill of a drain, and she realized she was trapped in a dead end. The crack didn't go anywhere. Of course it didn't. The only thing meant to come this way was filthy water.

Which did.

A hatch at shoulder level burst open between Cymbril and the hallway, the rim of a bucket tipped outward, and water gushed thunderously into the channel. She cringed as it splashed her, warm and fetid, flooding around her ankles.

"Is someone there?" said one of the women in the corridor, no more than eight paces away. Cymbril turned her hooded head just enough to gaze outward with one eye.

She'd seen the round-faced lady before—one of the Rake's richest, who controlled most of the pottery and glassware trade.

"How could there be someone there?" whispered the other lady, the one with the ornate fan. "What do you see?"

"Hello?" called the first, her smug face showing flickers of uncertainty.

She can't see me, Cymbril thought, glad she hadn't pulled forth her source of light. *I'm wrapped in a dark cloak.*

"Come along, Hysthia!" said the fan lady. "Unless, of course, your heart pines to meet some rogue in the shadows!"

But Hysthia would not be distracted. Her nostrils twitched, and her eyes bulged as she tipped her face left, then right. When she raised a bony, trembling hand as if to feel the darkness, Cymbril began to frown. Just whom—or what—did this jewel-draped woman think she had seen?

"It's—it's *her,*" Hysthia whispered. The rings on two fingers rattled together as her hand shook. She stared directly at Cymbril, all color gone from her face. The woman's free hand clutched her tasseled throw more tightly.

Cymbril narrowed her eye that was watching past the hood's edge.

"Whatever are you saying?" asked the fan lady.

"Her, I tell you—*her!* She won't stay in her grave. She'll never give me peace—she'll stop at nothing!" Hysthia's whole body quivered as if she were riding over a very rough road.

"Hysthia!" cried the other in alarm. "Seven saints!"

Then Hysthia sucked in her breath, and her eyes widened beyond what Cymbril would have thought possible. The woman's vision, Cymbril supposed, was beginning to adjust to the darkness. She was starting to make out a small, slender figure in the tight black space. And whatever that figure meant to her, it clearly filled her with horror.

The women weren't going away. There was nowhere to run—no chance for a peaceful retreat. As Cymbril saw it, there was nothing to do now but make an end in glory. Flinging her arms as wide as the walls would allow, spreading her cloak, she exerted all the power of her well-practiced voice.

Lunging toward Hysthia, voice like silver lightning, she screamed.

———

One level below, as Cymbril was later to hear in blistering detail, two sisters were laboring well into the evening. They were dyeing a batch of bed curtains in Moonpine, a hue blended in secret only on the Thunder Rake—a color famed for its evocation of moonlight in soft, needled boughs on summer nights; a dye prized for its indelible quality, its vivid brightness in the cloth even after years of launderings.

These sisters were twins named Gerta and Berta Curdlebree—wellborn, the daughters of a merchant family, but not particularly bright. Cymbril had felt sorry for them two years previously, when a peddler in an unremembered town had sold them a concoction promised to curl their hair into perfect ringlets. It had burned the hair completely from their heads, leaving the girls bald as eggs for several months.

Now, cap-free at last and relieved to have their unruly hair back, the sisters had been nearly finished with their appointed batch of curtains when a sound rent the air just over their heads: the cry of a banshee. In a wild fright, Gerta leaped toward her twin, though the drying line hung between them. A still-dripping curtain enfolded her.

Berta, for her part, reared away from the toppling blue cocoon. But Berta's escape was blocked by the bubbling pot in which the last curtain still steeped.

While Cymbril heard these details from Master Rombol, the sisters watched her without expression. Gerta's face and arms blossomed with patches of Moonpine blue that might have been bruises, though the bruises extended into and throughout her hair. Berta's feet rested on the softest footstool the Rake could produce; when the bandages came off, Cymbril was informed, the skin on Berta's feet and lower legs that was not newly regrown would also be the hue of the summer night sky.

And Hysthia Giltfeather, though thankfully still alive after the spasms her fright had induced, would not be traveling with the Rake this year. At her physician's advice, she had decided to take a long and quiet rest at her ancestral manor by the sea.

It was not the most auspicious beginning to a market season.

Chapter 2
The Urrmsh

The spring rains had come and gone. Fresh breezes and warmer air hardened the ground, making travel easier for the wheeled city. One by one, ships glided away down the long harbor of Whaleroad until their sails were small swatches of color on the horizon. Cymbril wished, as always, that she were hidden in one of the ships' holds, perhaps wrapped in an unsold carpet that might prove to be magical. At the first inviting island she passed, she would ride the carpet into the sky, racing with the gulls.

She sighed, turning from the rail. Carpets could not fly, and the only journey ahead of her was this one over land, for the annual cycle of selling. Her back ached, her knees stung from crawling on plank decks, and her hands were rough from soapy water. Since the incident outside the teabunk, she'd had an endless supply of floors to scrub. In her life thus far, she'd never noticed that the Rake was a city of floors upon floors, floors behind floors, always more floors.

When the sky turned to lavender, the feasting was exuberant. Raising goblets, the merchants made speeches in honor of hard work and prosperity, as if the getting of money were as lovely as the opening of buds on the boughs. Cymbril thought of the Setting-Out Feast as the "Feast of Greed."

For departure, Rombol always chose a night of the full moon, the shining disk in the sky symbolizing a coin. The feast began after moonrise with a ritual on the highest foredeck. Rombol would hold up an empty sack, open its neck to the moon, and shout:

> *Golden Moon, Magic Moon,*
> *Fill the vaults with treasure soon!*
> *May we all with able hands*
> *Earn the riches of the lands;*
> *Under sun and under clouds,*
> *Draw to Market mighty crowds;*
> *Send them home when all is told,*
> *Having given us their gold!*

And of course, Cymbril had to sing. Balancing on an oaken chest that served as her stage, she took request after request, her eyes stinging from the smoke, her stomach churning from the mingled odors of roast meat and spices, baked bread and wine, sweat and dog breath. This last was exuded by Bale, Master Rombol's lanky, enormous hound.

Bale would sidle among the tables, his head as high as the revelers' shoulders. He favored those he fancied with his glistening black nose under their arms, demanding a pat by flipping his neck—a powerful flip that could send a diner's cup or knife flying. All obliged him, some with coarse affection, some glancing nervously toward Rombol. With a *plotch, plotch, plotch* of his paws, Bale would approach Cymbril and stand motionless, his jowly snout raised. His sleepy, droopy eyes regarding her, he would sigh, a long expulsion of rancid heat that made her turn away and gasp for air.

When at last the feast was over, Cymbril bowed to those who clapped with greasy hands. She lifted her hem and carefully stepped down from the chest. Many merchants were already snoring, their heads on the tables in the flickering, oily light. As the clearers padded along the trestles, silent as ghosts, Cymbril moved to help them.

"That will do, Cymbril," called Master Rombol. Slouched

in his carved chair, he licked his fingers and wiped them on his black beard. He pointed at Cymbril with a chicken bone. "Go and rest your voice now. Tomorrow we roll into Highcircle, where the crowds await with their heavy purses!"

Several of the groggy merchants grinned.

"Be in your blue dress at first light." Rombol tossed the bone to Bale, who caught and crunched it in his jaws.

Cymbril curtsied and hurried into the corridor, thinking, *If you're worried about my voice, Master Rombol, why do you make me sing in the pipe smoke?* At least during market journeys, she could spend the day in fresh air, and by evening she had no voice left for the dining hall.

Shutting the door behind her, she leaned against it and inhaled the coolness. This hallway—called the Starpath, on the Rake's uppermost level—was a street tonight, its ceiling drawn back into the walls to let in the breeze and the light of the sky.

Cymbril tipped back her head, gazing up between walls at the uncountable bright stars—thousands of them, even in this thin strip of sky—so high above the world of masters and money. One of the Rake's cats rubbed against her ankles, and she knelt to stroke its fur. "It's Highcircle tomorrow, Miwa," Cymbril told the cat. "You'll have plenty of new mice to chase." Miwa purred, looking exactly as if she understood.

Her eyes glowed with the blue-green fire of the Fey world. Cats could always see the land of the Faeries, the Sidhe folk, side by side with the world of humankind. Cymbril fingered the stone in her skirt's pocket. She had a little of the Sidhe's fire, too.

Following the Starpath, she reached a square courtyard no more than ten paces across. At its center, a stone basin green with moss always held rainwater. It was full and clear after spring showers, brackish and murky by the end of summer, when it had collected dust, seedpods, and leaves blown from trees on the orchard deck towering just aft. Three closed doors led into different passageways. Cymbril liked to dip her hands into the water when it was fresh and cold. She admired how the pool reflected clouds in the daytime, stars at night.

But most of all, she enjoyed seeing the Monk's Door.

Long before, an artist had painted a picture on the door opposite the Starpath. Cymbril brushed it with her fingertips now—even in the starlight, the faded colors were visible. It showed a friar or monk with a gentle face, praying in a garden beneath a tree. The depiction had nothing to do with the corridor behind it, which led to the fruit bins and pruners' sheds. Cymbril knew of no other door on the Rake that bore a picture. It was only here, for reasons unknown, that some forgotten painter had chosen to preserve the image of a praying monk. And over the figure's tonsured head, twining among the leaves of trees, there were faint letters that read:

WISE IS THE ONE, AND TRULY FREE,
WHO MAKES A FRIEND OF AN ENEMY.

Cymbril smiled, because the words seemed so much at odds with what the Rake's merchants believed. She was certain Rombol had not ordered the painting done. Perhaps Rombol's father, the Rake's first master, had been a different sort of man than his son. She sat on the basin's mossy edge and petted Miwa, who purred and narrowed her eyes to glowing crescents.

But at the sound of the Overseer's horn, pulleys and chains began to move deep under the decks. Gears gnashed, axles creaked, and the Rake clawed the ground. The Thunder Rake rolled at night—daylight was for buying and selling. At the lurch of motion, Cymbril brightened. This was the hour she'd been waiting for all day. Far below, in the Pushpull Chamber, the benches were full again. After giving Miwa a final neck rub, she ran to the nearest crank basket and descended.

Cymbril pushed through a curtain of stringy brown vines. Dark and drippy, the room within was warm with many bodies, but it had none of the stuffiness of the dining hall. The Urrmsh occupied this long, narrow chamber, and of all the Thunder Rake's inhabitants, only the Urrmsh were content.

Even sitting on the rowing benches, they were taller than Cymbril, and as big around as boulders. Dark green and warty, they rocked back and forth, pushing and pulling on the "oars"—wooden levers that turned the gears that worked the Rake's tremendous claws, gouging the ground, drawing the vessel forward. The mouths and round eyes of the Urrmsh were like those of frogs. They had no ears, only nostril slits for noses, and short, thick legs. Most amazing were their muscular arms, so long they could reach to the floor, with hands that could crush a rock to powder. Humans, who generally had trouble trilling the *r* in "Urrmsh," also called them the Arm-folk or the Strongarms.

The Urrmsh smiled wide smiles as Cymbril passed between them, some pausing in their song to call her name or tap a fingertip on her head. She beamed and waved back, but she didn't try saying their names. Whenever she thought she'd learned them, the Armfolk changed places, rowing on different sides so that one arm wouldn't grow stronger than the other, and so that each rower could visit with a new bench-mate. The Urrmsh were nearly always singing, sometimes one by one, sometimes all together. The words were in their own language, which sounded something like the gurgle of rain through gutters, something like the purring of giant cats. "We sing our songs," they had explained to Cymbril. "We tell our tales, and we push and we pull. It is a good life."

One Strongarm she could always find was Urrt, because of his especially lumpy head, his lopsided smile, and his great size. He was several hundred years old—not at all old by Urrmsh standards. (None of the Armfolk kept a very careful count of their ages, though many of them remembered the world from when it was quite different.) Tonight Urrt was rowing on the right, at the very front. Cymbril threaded her way up the center aisle, stepping over the puddles that leaked from the canal above. The Strongarms liked to be wet. They glistened in the light from two rows of lanterns on strings.

There were just over three hundred of the Armfolk in the Pushpull Chamber, half on each side, two on each bench. The room itself lay in the center of the traveling city, deep in its cellars. Cymbril marveled that even this many rowers could move the Rake. It was a matter of levers, Urrt had told her—with a lever long enough, you could topple a mountain.

Cymbril settled in the dry front corner against a bulkhead, Urrt towering like a cliff above her. Pulling up her knees, she wedged her toes against the edge of his foot, its toenails cracked and yellow with age. He said nothing, but his gentle eyes watched her each time he rocked forward, his fingers locked on the limb-thick oar. When the song rolled toward Urrt, he sang, his deep voice resonating in the boards. Cymbril hummed on the same pitch.

She had always heard the tones of the world and had always answered them from within herself, matching the sound. As a very small girl, she'd stood in the middle of a deck and sung with the Rake. Her voice echoed the shriek of the axles, the roar of crowds, the stir of wind in leaves . . . and added something of her own, a nameless emotion that was both joy and loneliness, a cry that would not be stilled. When Rombol had determined that nothing ailed her, that she was singing like no child he'd ever heard, he found her a teacher of music and voice. Rombol knew a commodity when he heard one.

Now, sitting at Urrt's feet, Cymbril untied the silver twine from her hair, pulling free the jeweled pin. Her hair tumbled over her shoulders. Sliding the twine into her pocket, she withdrew the stone and laid her two treasures onto the table made by her skirt between her knees.

A stone from her father, a hairpin from her mother . . . but Cymbril had no faces to go with the words. Her mother and father had both died of the plague that swept the village where Cymbril had been born. After that, there had been an old woman who cared for her—or fed her, at least. Cymbril mostly remembered her red scarf and hairy chin. Then there was the Thunder Rake, and a woman of bony angles who'd taught Cymbril to sing. Selene—that was the woman's name. On the day Master Rombol sold Selene in Banburnish Crossing, Cymbril had learned that even people had prices. She'd understood then that Rombol wasn't her uncle or a charitable merchant who'd given her a home. He had bought her with shiny coins, just as people bought sacks of flour.

Cymbril held the hairpin between her fingers. The tiny jewel at its top absorbed and magnified whatever light was present—just now, the flickering pink of the Pushpull lanterns. In harmonious contrast, the smooth, flat, palm-size stone from her father always glowed with the blue-green fire of marsh lights, of cats' eyes, of the moon on a midnight sea. "Urrt," Cymbril said suddenly, trilling the *r* with practiced ease, "tell me again."

Urrt chuckled, the sound of rocks tumbling. "Never fear, little nightingale. You've heard it so often, you'll never forget." The thick oar lever passed back and forth over her head.

"Please tell me again. I like hearing it from you."

"Well, well," said Urrt, his voice hushed so as not to disturb the Strongarms' song—but the song echoed everywhere and could no more be disturbed than the earth's bones or oceans' tides. The song was not loud in the way that a crowd's roar was loud; it was more like the washing of waves on a sea coast, and quite conducive to sleep. "It is in the songs of the Urrmsh," Urrt said. "The stone is from your father and is the color of his eyes. The pin is from your mother and once adorned her hair. She was the most beautiful woman in the Misty Vales, and the sweetest singer, too. You, Cymbril, have her face and her voice." He glanced sideways at her with a full-moon eye. "Someday, little thrush, you must learn to sing in Urrmsh."

Cymbril smiled. The Urrmsh traveled everywhere. There were many others besides those on the Rake. In woods and swamps, on grassy hills, they gathered to exchange their songs. The music wove together news and wisdom in ways that made the important things hard to forget. Cymbril carefully let the treasures slip back and forth in the lap of her skirt—a bright circle, a pink spark. If she squinted, they looked like a firefly and the moon.

She was just beginning to feel drowsy when a long, braying tone resounded through the chamber, shattering the song. Wiltwain's horn again.

"Hooooo!" called the Strongarms together, and leaned back on their oars. Behind the walls, winches shuddered. Out in the night, the Rake's wheels ground to a halt. The steel claws plunged into the ground and rested.

Wiltwain the Overseer, Rombol's second in command, had blown the signal on his seashell trumpet. He appeared from the stairway, thrusting his sharp nose and chin through the moss curtain. "Just for a short bit, lads," he said, his glittering eyes sweeping the ranks of rowers. "We've got company coming aboard."

Company after sundown, and with the Rake only just having gotten under way. What could this mean? Cymbril stowed the treasures in her pocket, and when Wiltwain had gone, she sprang to her feet.

"See what it is, songbird," Urrt said. "But don't get stepped on."

Cymbril laid a hand on his enormous knuckle, smiled at him and his bench-mate, and dashed from the chamber. She sprinted up one quick turn of the spiral stairs to the high-arching avenue called Wagonhall, where the rolling tents and shops stood ready to stream down into Highcircle at daybreak. As she ran between the double row of waiting carts, her slippers pattering, she heard the measured rattle of the ramp's chains. It was most unusual for Rombol to lower the ramp after dark. The lands outside towns were haunted by robbers, wolves, and worse things—things that the old cooks whispered of in the scullery on winter nights, especially when they wanted to keep the younger girls from giggling around the banked hearth fires.

Hurrying forward with a shivery lightness in her chest, Cymbril wondered who—or what—might come up the ramp out of the night.

Chapter 3

Out of the Night and the Wild

Lantern light flared in the lofty hold ahead. There came a murmur of voices, the *thump* of the jointed ramp unfolding and striking the ground, and the neighing of horses. Rombol called a greeting to someone. On the first balcony, Cymbril worked her way forward among the silent carts, their wheels braced with wedges. Three more levels soared above, but Rombol and his party—a few merchants and a squad of armored guards—stood on the chamber's floor one story below, where the ramp slanted down into the dark outside the Rake. Cymbril eased into the driver's seat of the front wagon, its yoke set against the balcony rail.

Peeking over the footrest, she could see Rombol's group, but they weren't likely to see her . . . unless her hair glimmered.

Its gold did that in the glow of fires. After quickly gathering her hair, she jammed it down her collar and pulled the hood close around her face. Cymbril had learned to hide her head in order to avoid attention. People tended to stare at her startling blue eyes, her olive-golden skin, and, most of all, her shining hair— she simply didn't look like anyone else aboard the Rake.

Cloaked riders rumbled up into the hold, night mist swirling around the horses' hooves. Spurs glinted on muddy boots. Some riders had long bows across their backs. Sheathed swords were tucked beneath their knees, and their eyes shone watchfully in the shadows of their cowls. Cymbril counted seven strangers. They stayed in their saddles but guided their horses to the sides, making way for the eighth newcomer, a woman on a pale chestnut steed. She flung back her hood and shook her flowing hair.

Cymbril drew in her breath. The woman was not particularly tall, but she carried herself in a way that made her seem somehow larger than the rough men around her. A faint scar ran down her left cheek to the jaw. Her wide-set eyes fixed on Rombol. She did not smile.

It was more than her appearance, though, that held Cymbril transfixed. The silvery scar, the hard line of her mouth, her eyes—she seemed familiar in a haunting, inexplicable way. Surely Cymbril would have remembered meeting such a person. The strange thought that leaped into her mind was: *Maybe I dreamed her.*

"Brigit!" Rombol spread his arms as if greeting a close friend, but he kept his distance. "Welcome! The riders of the Lady honor us with their presence."

The woman—Brigit—gave a slow, imperious nod. "My Lady of the Wild has received your tribute and grants you favor for another year. You may come and go through her lands."

Rombol puffed out his chest and grinned in a way that showed no warmth. "That is good," he said.

Cymbril could hardly believe what she was hearing. She'd seen Rombol fawn before nobles, but never defer to a mud-booted woman who would not even get off her horse to speak to him. Cymbril sat completely still, trying to catch every word.

"But my visit now," Brigit continued, "does not concern my Lady Wildhair. It is an errand of my own. I bring news of your great good fortune."

Wildhair. Eyes wide, Cymbril nodded to herself. She'd heard of Wildhair, the fierce Huntress—Queen of the Witching Wild.

Rombol chuckled, hands on his barrel-like waist. "You hear news of me that I have not. What good fortune is mine?"

"The fortune of the purchase you are about to make."

Brigit signaled one of her riders, who prodded his black horse forward. Cymbril had thought the rider was a fat man, but when he shrugged open his cloak, she saw that he'd been concealing a small, slender person on the saddle before him.

Cymbril stared. It was a boy unlike any she'd ever seen. He had a long, beautiful face, a tiny mouth, and shoulder-length hair precisely the color of the moon. He wore a gray tunic that rippled like the swirling patterns of a stream.

Rombol had begun to laugh at Brigit's words, but the sound snagged in his throat. For a full count of five, he gawked at the boy.

At last Brigit showed the hint of a smile. "Yes. It's a Fey child. A Sidhe. They're not at all easy to catch. But he'll be worth the price."

Rombol blinked. Like a man waking from a daydream, he glanced at his fellow merchants. "Worth it? How?"

Brigit's horse snorted, almost as if expressing scorn at Rombol's ignorance.

"They can see in the dark, for one thing," Brigit said. "With these eyes on your prow, you'll be able to run the Rake from Fencet to Ardle, straight through the Groag Swamp. A single night, open for business in the dawn. I believe you tried it once before and broke two wheels."

One of her riders snickered.

A gray-haired merchant spoke up—old Crenlaw, who seemed not to care if he offended the riders. "Do you take us for fools, Brigit? It's impossible to keep one of the Elder folk as a prisoner for very long. The birds of the air are all spies for the Sidhe. This boy's people will come to get him. We've no mind to make enemies of elfin enchanters."

Brigit's eyes shone in the torch fire like those of a fox. Again something flashed in Cymbril's memory, beyond her reach—a dark mirror deep in her mind that reflected the light of those eyes, then was dark once more.

"Master Rombol's not worried about that," Brigit said. "The old spells of protection guarding this Rake are still strong, though the hand that cast them is gone. Your rolling city is safe from Fey magic." Craftily, she added, "Only numbers and skill at arms could overwhelm you."

Some of Rombol's group bristled. Cymbril understood Brigit was reminding them that only Wildhair deserved their fear. If Brigit were a mere message-bearer for the Lady, what must the Huntress herself be like—she who ruled the deepest woods where the King's soldiers seldom passed?

Rombol licked his lips. " 'For one thing,' you said. What else can this boy do?"

Brigit nudged her horse forward. When she was looming above the Rake's Master, she leaned closer with an elbow on her knee. "I think I need say no more except this: a thousand pieces of gold."

Rombol's lip curled. "Seven hundred. He looks sickly."

"A Sidhe child is worth a thousand and a half. I'm being generous."

"You're never generous. Eight."

The horse swished its tail. Brigit raised her eyebrows, using the power of her pale stare, her mounted height, and silence. Cymbril had never seen anyone bargain so impertinently with Rombol—and in the porch of the Rake itself, at night. She couldn't help admiring this woman for whom the city had stopped in its tracks.

"I'll wait for a lower price," said Rombol. "Who else would you sell him to? Only the King himself could pay what you ask."

Brigit blinked languidly. "I could find other buyers— less worthy of the purchase, but with gold just as good as yours. But you can afford nine hundred."

Rombol looked around his group and then again at the boy, who stared back, his mouth getting even smaller.

"Eight-fifty, fair and done," said Rombol. "But first, we see him walk and hear him talk." He sent his vault keeper for the gold.

The man on the black horse lowered his light-haired

charge to the deck. Cymbril thought the boy looked about her age—twelve, no more than thirteen—if the Sidhe aged like humans. His dust-colored trousers were torn and muddy, his long, rippling shirt bound at the waist with a silver rope. His boots seemed stitched of leaves and made no sound as he walked slowly toward Rombol. Shoulders square, he gazed up at the merchant. If the boy was afraid, he didn't show it.

Brigit watched without expression, but Cymbril noticed one hand near her sword hilt.

Cymbril held her breath. Did Brigit expect treachery from the Rake's merchants? No—the woman was focused on the boy. *She's afraid of him,* Cymbril thought. *She doesn't like even letting him walk a few steps free.*

The boy looked so slight and fragile, especially standing before Rombol—a candlestick before a bear.

"What are you called?" Rombol demanded.

"I am Loric, New Master." The boy spoke with a lilting accent, as if the words of humans felt strange in his mouth.

" 'New Master'?" Rombol gripped the boy's shoulder and shook him jovially. "Well said, Loric. Remember that, and you'll do splendidly here. Forget it, and you'll be sorry."

The money was brought and counted, piece by piece, from one bag to another. Loric's eyes followed the flash of each gold coin. When Rombol glared at him suspiciously, the boy returned his New Master's gaze with rapt attention. "Do not stare," growled Rombol. "Do not look me or anyone in the eye. And do not look at what is not yours."

Loric closed his eyes tightly and stood still as a tree.

"What are you doing, boy?"

"Nothing around me is mine, New Master. I cannot look at anything."

Rombol's thick hand twitched, and Cymbril was sure he was about to strike the boy for impertinence. But instead the Master leaned close to Loric's face. "Don't be a fool," he rumbled quietly. "Open your eyes."

Loric did so, looking confused, and bowed from the neck. "I will try to learn your ways quickly," he said.

"Hmm," said Rombol, gnawing his lip as he straightened to watch the Fey through squinted eyes.

"In another day," said Brigit, wheeling her horse around, "you'll wonder how you managed without him." She lingered at the top of the ramp, surveying the group a final time. "Tread lightly in Wolfhome, in the lonely places. My Lady is watching. Until we meet again." She charged away, leading her party into the dark. Loric raised a hand in farewell, but none of the riders looked at him.

Old Crenlaw peered down from the ramp's top. When the hoofbeats had faded, he made a show of coughing up phlegm and spitting it noisily after them.

A merchant turned Loric around. "Do you sleep, Fey boy?"

"Yes," said Loric. "I'm very tired now."

They ushered him away, fingering his hair and shirt, exclaiming how rare he was. Soon the doors were shut, and silence returned to the hold.

The Rake shuddered and began again to roll.

Cymbril sat for a long time on the wagon's footboards, hugging her knees, restless. If only the red-scarfed woman long ago had sold her to Wildhair instead of Rombol, she could be galloping away now with the riders, the night wind in her hair. In her mind she wove a dream in which Brigit was her cousin, teaching her to shoot arrows from the saddle.

Chapter 4

The Peace Offering

Cymbril usually awoke at the sound of Wiltwain's horn signaling the Armfolk—or if not then, nearly always when the Rake stopped moving. But the morning of the arrival in High-circle, she sat up with a start at the shouting of merchants. The Rake sat motionless, and beyond the walls of her cramped bunk, she could hear people hauling sacks and wheeling carts in the wooden avenues. It must be nearly sunrise! Snatching her hairbrush, she scrambled from beneath her frayed cover and tumbled barefoot into the hall, the floorboards cool with early summer. A few of the other maidservants were still at the kettles, where coals burned in an iron pit and steam rose through the ceiling hatch into a rosy sky.

Cymbril splashed warm water over her arms and face,

scrubbed with the gritty gray soap, and pulled the brush through her hair. Then she dashed back to her chamber to wriggle into the blue dress. She hated its sleeves, puffy at the shoulders and so tight around the wrists that they were impossible to roll up. The sleeves also had brocaded points that came down the backs of her hands as if to show her where her fingers were. She straightened her hair again, dropped her treasures into her waist pocket, and hurried to line up in the ramp hold.

On the first balcony above, her hiding place of the previous night was crowded with horses and drivers. Chickens clucked, goats bleated, and masters barked at slaves. Crafters, tailors, cooks, and peddlers waited to descend on Highcircle, where even fine lords and ladies attended the Rake's market.

One of the seamstresses shoved a basket of pincushions into Cymbril's arms, muttering, "Make yourself useful." Cymbril stretched onto her toes, looking for Loric. In the typical morning bustle, she began to wonder if she'd only dreamed him.

But there he was, dressed in the same water-gray shirt and a new pair of trousers. A heavy iron collar encircled his neck, half-hidden by his hair. A chain dangled behind him, its end fastened to another manacle locked around Rombol's belt. Loric turned this way and that, his attention captured by each new person or cartload he saw.

"Stand still," grumbled Rombol.

Studying the chain and collar, Cymbril frowned. She'd heard blacksmiths boast that all worked metal was poisonous to the Fey folk, that its very touch burned their skin like flame. Yet Loric seemed hardly to notice the shackling.

When the block wardens had counted all the servants and reported to Wiltwain, Rombol marched to the ramp and lifted his arms. He wore a red velvet cape and a matching hat like a tea cozy, and he carried a cane with a silver goose's head. "A perfect day!" he bellowed. On the soaring balconies and the grand floor around him, his people cheered. Their shouts and applause startled birds from the rafters. Loric cringed and covered his ears. The gate crashed down. Then the carts' wheels turned, and Loric was nearly yanked off his feet. The merchants trooped after the silver goose head as if following the King's banner.

Puffs of cloud hung in the mildest blue sky anyone might hope for. Clumps of violets and clover spread like vibrant quilts on both sides of the path. Sleepy cattle watched from the shadows of trees by a watering hole. The air was alive with fragrance and light. Cymbril drew a deep breath. It was wonderful to be outdoors, even with the basket in her arms.

Highcircle's crowds were already waiting. Children and dogs ran alongside the merchants' wagons as they trundled from the meadow to the wide market ground. Women in white bonnets murmured and pointed. Servants in feathered caps came from the houses of the rich with long lists of supplies to buy. On the hilly road that led up to the castle, one of the Knights of the Fountains sat astride his charger and raised a gauntlet at Rombol's flourish of a bow. Always when she glimpsed a knight, Cymbril wondered if it might be the one she'd met before, in the summer when she was eight—the one and only time she'd been on a horse's back.

Tent stakes sank into the mud; blocks again wedged the carts' wheels. Pavilions rose in the sun's early rays. Carpets and flags unfurled.

Cymbril wandered absently after Rombol and the Sidhe boy as the throng she'd been with dispersed, each person having a place to be and a job to do. She was looking around for the seamstress when someone spoke beside her.

"What have you got there?"

Cymbril blinked, peering at a large-boned girl with a bonnet pulled oddly down around her face and tied beneath her chin. The girl was a few years older than Cymbril, and there was something strange about her complexion. Her cheeks and chin looked shadowy, as if the bright sunlight somehow couldn't reach her.

With a start, Cymbril recognized her, and realized that the girl's skin was blue. Moonpine blue—Gerta. And on

Cymbril's other side was Berta, wearing no bonnet, but hobbling slightly.

A rush of apologies tangled in Cymbril's mind. She opened her mouth, looking from sister to sister.

"Pincushions," said Berta, snatching one out of the basket. "Did you make them?"

"Bet it took you a long time," said Gerta.

"No, I—" Cymbril began.

"Going to sell them?" demanded Gerta, raising purplish eyebrows. "Didn't know you could sew."

"She can't," said Berta with a sniff. "These aren't very good. But we can fix that, can't we, Gert?"

Gerta, before Cymbril could get a word in edgewise, pulled a bottle from her pocket and tugged out the stopper.

Cymbril yelped and turned away her face, but the girl was aiming at the basket. Gerta dumped the bottle's contents over the pincushions. Moonpine dye spurted. Cymbril jumped backwards, but Berta seized the basket, yanking it out of Cymbril's grasp. Both sisters danced, emptying the bottle, their laughter like the braying of donkeys.

At a safe distance, Cymbril could only gape—as much at the sisters' choice of location as at their cruelty. This wasn't revenge in some dark hallway. It was the middle of a market, under the sun. They truly had no sense at all.

The seamstress, having seen the whole encounter, pounced on the Curdlebree twins. Inarticulate with rage, she seemed unsure whether to box the girls' ears or use them as handles to drag them away to justice—so she inflicted a pummeling.

Gerta and Berta howled, pointing uselessly at Cymbril as they dodged blows and began to shove each other.

When the three had whirled away, the seamstress now having a firm grip on the sisters' wrists, Cymbril stood gasping for breath, the blue-dyed pincushions scattered around her feet like a harvest of strange fruit. She felt as if she'd narrowly missed being run over by a wagon.

Using a weed's broad leaf to keep the dye off her fingers, she refilled the basket. She'd just finished when Wiltwain tapped her shoulder. He frowned at the basket but was too busy to ask. "There," the Overseer said, pointing. "Stand on that wagon bed. Sing us 'The Skylark' and then 'The Bells of Avernon.'"

Cymbril pointed at the basket. "What should I—?"

"Is it your basket?"

Vehemently, Cymbril shook her head no.

Wiltwain rolled his eyes. "Then leave it there." He clapped his hands for haste. "The sun doesn't wait."

Cymbril didn't feel the least bit like singing. Taking care not to drag her hem, she circled the worst of the mud and climbed into the now-empty wagon. Even before she opened her mouth, a crowd was gathering. Wiltwain was announcing her, and the folk of Highcircle remembered her. "The Thrush!" someone shouted. "The Thrush of the Thunder Rake!"

She filled her lungs with the fresh field-scented breeze and sang. Her voice spread like the growing light, and even people at the ground's far end stopped their bargaining and turned to listen. Her eyes strayed to Rombol and Loric, over near the bakers' tents, where a woman and two girls were running their fingers through Loric's hair. Twice Cymbril sang the wrong words, and she saw Wiltwain give her a scowl. Then she'd finished "The Skylark," and the crowd was whistling and shouting requests. She shut her eyes, curled her hands into fists beneath the blue dress's wretched sleeve points, and sang.

For all the discomfort of being forced to sing on demand, once she'd started, Cymbril loved to make music with her voice. She found delight in the deep breathing, in shaping the words and tones. Sometimes it was like painting pictures in the air with a soft brush; other times it was like throwing lightning bolts that dazzled and crashed. When she sang, she was not a slave—she could be anyone: a queen, a soldier, a forlorn lover. She could be no one at all but the timeless voice of music, integral to everything.

Yet she could never stay long in that place beyond markets and masters. When she was allowed to rest, Highcircle's women swarmed around her as they always did, cupping her chin and declaring how pretty she was. Cymbril imagined herself spitting at them and scratching their warty cheeks.

Amid the babble and the blur of faces, the smudging of hands and the stink of breath, Cymbril shut her ears, retreating into the silence of her mind as if hiding in a well. But a child's high-pitched voice pulled her back. "Mama! She looks like the elf boy! Is she his sister?"

Cymbril focused her gaze.

"No, Haddie." A woman grasped Cymbril's hair and shoved her curly-headed child so close that Cymbril put up her arms to avoid a collision. "See? She's a girl like your sister. See? Her skin isn't as white as the elf's, and her eyes don't shine like his."

Elf boy. Sister. Why would the child say that? She peered through the crowd toward Loric, who was standing patiently in a tangle of admirers. Cymbril's heart leaped strangely when she saw that his brown eyes were fixed on her.

Not sure what to do, she smiled.

With a serious expression, he bowed from the neck. How polite he was. Couldn't he tell Cymbril was a slave like himself? Because of her expensive dress, did he think she was a merchant's daughter? The idea that he might think so bothered her. She would have to set him straight.

Cymbril had forgotten just how endless market days felt. Back on the Thunder Rake at last, she was given time to take a full bath, and the laundresses whisked away the pale blue dress. Cymbril was thankful to have escaped Gerta's dousing of Moonpine blue, but she wouldn't have minded a bit if that dress got ruined. Maybe the laundresses would have an accident with lye.

Profits had exceeded Rombol's expectations, and it was decided that the Rake would stay another day in Highcircle. That meant the Armfolk had a night and a full day off. They all made a slow trek into the forests to splash in the streams, doze on the moss, and learn new parts for their songs. That in turn meant Cymbril couldn't talk to Urrt or any of the others, for she was never permitted off the Rake alone.

As she was helping to wash the supper dishes and thinking she was too tired to do her nightly skulk-about, someone called her name. Drying her hands, she saw the seamstress—the one who had given her the pincushions to carry.

Cymbril braced herself for a scolding, but the weary-looking woman only wanted to hear her version of what Gerta and Berta had against Cymbril. The seamstress listened, ringleted gray head cocked to one side, hands on her ample waist, as Cymbril related the story of her scream—though, in her telling, the scream had been one of terror when Hysthia Giltfeather had cornered her in the drain channel and reached for her with long, clawed fingers. If the seamstress wanted a completely factual account of the crime, Cymbril reasoned, she shouldn't be asking the culprit.

"So that's where the dyed face and the burned feet came from," said the seamstress. "You didn't attack them in their workshop."

Cymbril widened her eyes. "Is that what they said?"

The woman sighed and tapped a finger on Cymbril's forehead. "Give thanks on your knees, girl, that you're sound up here. Those poor twins aren't right upstairs, and no one will give them the time of day. Sad thing is, they weren't always like that."

"What do you mean?" Cymbril asked. "What happened to them?"

The seamstress shook her head. "No one can say. They're healthy as oxen, never had the fever or the pox. But when they were small, they were bright as new buttons. It's as if their minds are just withering away. I swear they're worse now than they were last year!"

When she'd gone, Cymbril wandered slowly back toward her bunk, deep in thought. The notion of clever girls becoming as dull and strange as the Curdlebree twins disturbed her. At times when she was troubled, it helped to remember things she'd learned from the Urrmsh. They were creatures of endless patience and peace. Whenever Cymbril sang, she thought she understood their calm spirits and their joy at being alive. But that morning, looking into the eyes of the Curdlebree sisters, she'd seen such unhappiness. *No one gives them the time of day,* Cymbril told herself. *If they have some illness of the mind, life has been unfair to them. They're lonely. They're angry at me for dyeing and burning them.*

The reason for that anger had been Cymbril's fault. She couldn't deny the fact that her mischievous impulse to scare Hysthia Giltfeather had injured the twins. The rankling unease she felt in her chest was guilt. Even after their act of hatred, ruining the pincushions—even then, watching the seamstress box them, Cymbril had felt guilty.

She stopped walking and folded her arms. All at once, she remembered the words from the Monk's Door.

WISE IS THE ONE, AND TRULY FREE,
WHO MAKES A FRIEND OF AN ENEMY.

She didn't exactly want friendship from the Curdle-brees. Nothing she'd ever heard them say appealed to her in the least, and she must be equally uninteresting to them. But Cymbril resolved to make amends if she could. She didn't want Gerta and Berta as enemies, and if possible, she would find a way to bring them a little of the peace that the Urrmsh felt.

It wouldn't be easy.

But she had an idea. She knew someone—well, sort of someone—who would give Gerta and Berta the time of day. Her tiredness retreated.

Yes, a skulk-about was in order, after all.

When the block was quiet, Cymbril hurried by the side corridors to a dim, unnamed branch off Tinley, where there was a row of three storage rooms. Their heavy iron-banded doors were kept locked, but crawling around between levels when she was seven or eight, Cymbril had found a way to come down inside the chambers from above. Each had a ceiling hatch and a ladder that seemed once to have connected with an upper story; but a new deck had been built over their tops, leaving only a cobwebby space just big enough to creep through on hands and knees.

At first, Cymbril had been afraid of the rooms and avoided them for several years. A dusty mirror in the first chamber had unsettled her. Nor did she like certain disturbingly shaped pieces of furniture beneath moth-eaten cloth. The second room was packed floor to ceiling with trunks and boxes, all locked or bound with chains that Cymbril had never cared to try undoing. But the third held a jumble of more accessible objects: lenses on hinged arms, rolled-up maps, glass bottles in an array of colors and designs, books and tins, barrels of metal parts.

Rombol had seen to it that Cymbril knew her letters early in life, for many of the songs she might sing were written down. But unlike most books, the ones crowding the shelves in the locked room and stacked to its ceiling in places didn't appeal to her. Most were in other languages, and some held nothing but numbers and shapes. The pages smelled musty— and some had worse odors, as if they'd been doused with chemicals or kept in a cupboard where food had rotted. Nearly all the tomes, on the first leaf inside the cover, had been embossed with a stylized letter *R*, which Cymbril assumed must stand for Rombol. When she had come to a leather-bound volume filled with drawings of terrible monsters, she snapped it shut and gave up on the books.

A far better discovery had awaited on a small round table covered with a fringed cloth. Centered on the table sat a beautifully carved wooden box. Fancy letters across its top spelled what Cymbril assumed was a name: BYRNI.

On the night of her peacemaking mission, she climbed down through the hatchway and descended the ladder into the third storage chamber. Moving by the light of her blue-green stone, she threaded her way among the stacks and crates, noting that nothing ever appeared to change in the room—never anything missing, never any new additions. She doubted anyone but herself had entered during her whole lifetime.

Yes, Byrni was still present, the box and the rich purple tablecloth gray with dust. The first time Cymbril had opened the box, carefully snapping back its latches, she'd had quite a start—not so much because of what Byrni was, but because she hadn't expected him to *speak*. But she'd been much younger then. Now, she told herself, she would hardly blink at discovering such a thing.

For Byrni—if indeed that was his name—was a talking

skull. A human skull, and quite real, he nestled face-upward on a plush velvet cushion, and his jaw waggled up and down as he spoke. Cymbril supposed it was the gentleness of his voice and the steady monotony of what he said that had kept her from being afraid. The fact was, Byrni *never* stopped talking. Cymbril didn't converse with him, because Byrni did not listen—always, he talked. It was clearly an instance of magic. For reasons unknown, some magician long ago had cast a spell on the skull.

Cymbril knew that Byrni kept talking when the box was closed—though it was perfectly soundproof—because she'd experimented by closing and reopening the lid, listening to the flow of the sentences, noticing their progress. Byrni talked of history and geography—lineages of kings, mountains in order from west to east, from lowest to highest. He listed birds and fish and herd animals, land by land. He discoursed on capitals and trade and fruit and shipbuilding, weather and stars, winds and sands. Apparently, he knew everything there was to know. His speech was nothing but facts—nothing so interesting as stories—so Cymbril never listened for long.

Once she'd carefully lowered a wadded cloth into his mouth. He'd jabbered right on, though his words had been muffled until she pulled it out again. As far as she could tell, he didn't mind when she closed the box, but he always interrupted himself to greet her when she opened it.

She supposed Byrni was a broken talking skull. Maybe once he'd been an invaluable resource, lying quietly on his cushion and only spouting exactly the information requested. Perhaps one day the magician had accidentally dropped him or asked a question to which there was no answer, and Byrni had begun his everlasting speech. Then he'd been relegated to this storage room. It puzzled Cymbril that Rombol left these store-rooms alone. There must be priceless treasures here—Byrni, for one. Byrni was wearisome but unquestionably valuable.

Just to check that the talking skull was safe, she undid the latches and raised the lid.

"Ah!" said Byrni pleasantly. "So good to see you! As I was saying: Jehachel had four sons, and, for the purpose at hand, I will speak of the third, a fair-haired boy called Mihal, commonly known for his part in—"

Unceremoniously, Cymbril closed the box, wrapped it in a fold of her cloak, and tucked it under her arm, taking care not to jostle Byrni. She'd borrowed him once before, when she'd smuggled him into the Pushpull Chamber and lent him to the Urrmsh for two days, thinking that his unending stream of facts might be useful to them in their song making. It had not gone over too well. Byrni's voice did not carry far in the dripping, creaking chamber, so the Urrmsh had been obliged to row in silence, without the entertainment of their songs.

And those within earshot of Byrni had kept dozing off, which never happened when the Armfolk were left to their own devices. Though they'd kept him hidden from Wiltwain by sliding the box under a bench, the Overseer had been suspicious at the two-day lack of Strongarm singing. In the end, Burrub—marginally less polite to Cymbril than Urrt ever was— begged her to throw Byrni overboard, or at least to take him back where she'd found him.

Cymbril wasn't so naive as to think Byrni would be an actual friend to Gerta and Berta. But he was interesting in small doses.

It was no small feat getting unnoticed to the door of the quarters where the sisters lived with their mother. Hallways in the merchants' blocks flickered with lantern light even in the quiet watches, and men-at-arms made frequent patrols. Although the large sums of gold were in the Rake's vaults, the merchants kept their day-to-day market strongboxes in their dwellings. Still, Cymbril knew the back ways and crawlspaces as well as many of the Rake's cats did, and in a short while she emerged from a stairwell, counted doors, checked a brass nameplate, and set Byrni's box down softly before the sisters' front portal.

If the twins or their mother saw Cymbril herself, there would probably be unpleasantness. Therefore, Cymbril had neatly lettered a note on a square of parchment, which she laid atop the box. It said:

For Gerta and Berta Curdlebree. I'm very sorry about the scream, the dye, and burning your feet. Here's someone I borrowed from the storeroom for you, for a while. I'll have to take him back in a few days, but he'll be glad if you give him some attention. Don't be alarmed. Please accept my apologies.

—Cymbril

She gnawed her lip, studying the box, and pushed it a little closer to the dwelling.

With a prickling sensation in the back of her neck, she was suddenly certain that someone was watching her. She straightened, her heart pounding, and peered right and left. No one was about. The dancing flames in the lamps were all that moved. But still, she felt eyes upon her, and it made her scalp tingle. Who was watching? And from where?

Then she saw, near the floor of a shadowy alcove, a pair of luminous round eyes in a dark silhouette. Cymbril let out a slow breath, feeling relief and annoyance. The eyes stared at her without blinking. They belonged to a frog she had often seen—a hideous, bloated frog that hopped all over the Rake, living off the beetles and many-legged worms it caught with a *splat* of its sticky tongue. The frog was obscenely large, the size of a small footstool, bigger than any frog Cymbril had seen. She didn't like it when the vile creature watched her. But watching was what it nearly always did, from beneath stairways, from the puddles under the canal deck. *Go away,* she told the frog silently. *Find someone else to stare at.*

She turned back to the box. Having straightened the note on top, she rapped sharply on the door five times and walked quickly back to the concealment of the stairwell.

Peeping around the corner, she watched, her heart racing.

In a moment the door clicked and opened a crack. Then it swung wider, and Gerta's head emerged, blinking in the lantern light as she looked up and down the corridor. Even in the dimness, the blue blotches were still plainly visible. Since she wore no bonnet now, the disarray of her hair gleamed yellow and blue, like a hayfield partly in the shade of clouds.

Above Gerta's head, Berta's protruded. Her hair was tied up in many tiny strips of cloth.

Cymbril held her breath.

Gerta reached down and picked up the note. Oddly, she turned the parchment over and looked at its back, frowning. Cymbril watched closely, but the girl's only reaction seemed puzzlement.

"Someone left a box," Gerta said.

Not someone, Cymbril shouted in her mind. *Me! Read the note!*

"Is anyone there?" Berta called.

Shhh, Cymbril thought. *You'll wake the whole block.*

Stooping, Gerta lifted the box, half crushing the note against it, and carried it inside. Berta took a last look right and left, then shut the door.

Good, Cymbril thought. *That's that. Now I hope we're straightened out, and bygones are bygones.* Letting out a long breath, she dried her palms on her skirt and turned to go.

Then came a bloodcurdling shriek.

Cymbril whirled around.

A second voice was added to the first, screaming.

Cymbril's knees went weak, and she clutched the wall.

On a slightly lower, hoarser pitch, rose a third voice—the girls' mother.

Then the door flew open, and Gerta burst into the corridor in her nightgown. As she sprinted in the direction away from Cymbril, her cry broke up into words: "It talks, it talks, it talks, it talks!"

An instant later Berta followed her sister, hands flailing around her head as if she were tearing her way through spider webs. "Ahh! It's HORRIBLE!"

About the time more doors began swinging open and other wide-eyed heads poked into the corridor, the twins' mother lurched from the doorway, ran two steps in one direction, three in another, and then collapsed in a swoon.

Cymbril sank against the wall, covering her face, and slid down until she was sitting on her heels, telling herself, *"Don't be alarmed," I wrote. I wrote, "Don't be alarmed."*

Men and women raced up and down the hallway. A bristle-bearded man with a longsword dashed in through the open door of the twins' quarters, likely suspecting thieves.

He reemerged, screaming.

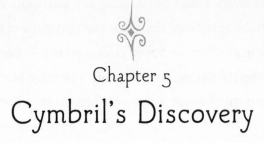

Chapter 5

Cymbril's Discovery

Cymbril knew it would be a very long night. There was no way to avoid whatever wrath and punishment were coming. She'd signed her name to the evidence of her crime. Not waiting around for the guards to catch her—and not caring to be dragged from her bunk—she doubled back by the canal, flitted like a forlorn ghost across the Mermaid Bridge, and stole up Grandway, straight into the garrison square.

Rombol had a high-backed chair there, its arms and feet carved into dragon claws, perched in a bed of moonthistles that could grow without light. When disputes needed settling or a criminal had to be judged, the Rake's Master occupied the chair, before the three doors of the main barracks. On a platform in one corner of the square were the stocks, a frame of heavy timbers with holes cut for a prisoner's neck, wrists, and ankles—a single set, since it was rare for any of the Rake folk to do anything deserving of the stocks. In this rolling city, everyone was registered and accounted for. No strangers drifted through. The merchants shared a common purpose like the crew of a ship, their community locked within a hull of impenetrable timbers, isolated by surroundings that constantly changed. Crime and disruptions were rare—a fact that made catastrophes like this present one all the worse.

Cymbril gazed pensively at the stocks, thinking that she'd never been in them but that this would probably be the night. The platform's steps squeaked beneath her slippers. She touched the iron padlock, the rough boards. A cricket was fiddling in the thistles. Cymbril closed her eyes and tried to calm the nervous tremors in her stomach. Something pressed against her ankle, and she looked down to see Miwa the cat, purring and circling as if to comfort her. Stooping, she scooped up Miwa and cradled her in both arms, leaning against the stocks. "I think I've really done it this time," she whispered into the cat's ear. Miwa squinted and tilted her head back for a neck rub. Absently, Cymbril wondered how old Miwa was. She seemed nimble and spry, but she'd been around for as long as Cymbril could remember. At times Cymbril could swear she'd known Miwa even before coming aboard the Rake—but that, of course, was unlikely.

Feet hammered up Grandway. A lone guard raced across the square, clutching the sheathed sword at his hip to keep it from tripping him. Dashing past Cymbril, he was nearly to the first barracks' door when he realized whom he'd just seen and skidded to a stop. Whirling, he stared up at Cymbril and pointed with an unsteady hand.

"You." He tried to sound stern, but all he sounded was out of breath. "You're to see the Master at once."

Cymbril nodded, letting Miwa gently down. "Where?"

The guard opened his mouth and frowned, blinking. Clearly, he hadn't planned on finding her so easily and had come to rouse the garrison and begin scouring the Rake for her, deck by deck. He aimed his finger at her again, but still nothing came from his lips.

Cymbril knew the Master was extremely private about his own quarters, where he would normally be at this hour. None of his orders or reprimands were ever delivered there— which was why she'd come to his dragon chair. "Perhaps you should go and look for him," she suggested. "I'll wait."

The guard had the good sense to pound on the door and

summon two men-at-arms, whom he charged to watch Cymbril.

The soldiers looked sleepy, but since they'd appeared quickly in full battle dress, with shields and pole arms, she supposed they were on duty, making occasional patrols. One scratched his head and then sat on the wooden stairs, donning and buckling his helmet. The other spit on a scuffed patch of his breastplate and buffed it with his sleeve. Fixing a watery eye on Cymbril, he leaned on his halberd. "So, what cha done this time, little miss?"

Rombol stormed into the square, his hair in a matted disarray, his cloak billowing around him. The guards snapped to attention. Saying nothing, Rombol headed for the nearest door into the barracks and, with the twirl of a hooked finger, commanded Cymbril to come along. He carried a bundle under one arm, in which she guessed was Byrni.

The Master threw open the door and snatched a burning torch from a wall sconce inside. Having entered a room on the right, he set the torch in a bracket. When Cymbril had scampered in after him, he shoved the door closed with a crash.

He hulked against the door, his head nearly touching

the ceiling. At each breath through his pitted red nose, he rumbled. Cymbril felt she was in a cave with a bear that she'd just kicked awake.

The small room held only a table and a chair. Cymbril put the chair in front of her and clung to its back, hoping her knees wouldn't give way. She tried to keep her face blank as Rombol dropped the bundle onto the tabletop. Her heart seemed to have risen into her throat, but she was determined to justify herself. She'd had the best of intentions.

"You," Rombol said finally, in a quiet, dark voice. "It's always you. When I'm yanked awake from the sweetest dreams, when hard-working folk run and scream in the night—it's always you they're running from." He clutched the top of her head with a broad palm and stared into her eyes. "Are you Cymbril or some fairy in disguise?"

Cymbril bit her lip, determined not to wither.

The Master released her head. "And if you are Cymbril, did some witch or devil send you to haunt this Rake?"

"I was trying to make things right," she began earnestly. "I thought—"

Rombol held up a hand for silence. "I've read your missive. Oh, how happy I am I taught you to write! It triples your capacity for mischief."

Cymbril kept her gaze averted.

He pointed at the bundle. "Where did you get that?" he demanded.

She tried not to let her surprise show. Rombol didn't know where Byrni had come from? How could he not—he who knew every latch and girandole, who accounted for every button and doorstop in his lists?

"From the storeroom," she said. "The one by Tinley that no one ever goes into."

"Except you, apparently." A look she could not identify passed over Rombol's face. "What storeroom?"

She spread her arms, not knowing how else to describe it. "The one with the magician's things and those old, scary books of yours, stamped with an R."

"Show me." Rombol snatched up the bundle, his eyes wide. "Take me there."

They made one stop at his quarters. Cymbril waited in the hall as the Master went in and emerged with his great ring of keys. Then they hurried through the avenues, Cymbril free for once to take the most direct, public ways. Now and then they saw a patrolling guard who saluted Rombol, and at the mouth of Hyacinth, they met old Spargulus the lamp warden, with his taper and his flask of oil.

All the way, Cymbril thought of the undisturbed dust on the storeroom's floor—a room where such odd things were kept—and of Rombol's strange reaction.

They took Longwander to Tinley and passed beneath the dark, abandoned chandelier of angels, a cobwebby monstrosity that dangled forever in a ceiling well formed by the arrangement of half-levels above. Cymbril began counting hallways that led away to the left. When she reached the proper one and turned into it, Rombol stood still and gaped.

Cymbril peered at him curiously. A draft made the nearest lamp waver, casting shadows across his face. He looked up and down Tinley, at the ceiling above, and into the narrow, nameless corridor of the three storerooms. When he crouched and used his knife to carve an X into the planks of Tinley, Cymbril understood.

"You've never seen this hallway before," she said quietly.

Rombol made no answer.

Magic. There had to be magic at work, hiding the corridor even from the Rake's Master. *Of course*—now it made sense why no one went into the storerooms and why such wondrous relics were left untouched in the dark. Maybe the musty books didn't belong to Rombol after all. But how could the hallway be secret? Countless times Cymbril had heard the

Master boast of how his father Tycho had ordered the Rake built and had organized the guild of merchants, of whom he was the richest and the chief—and Rombol was his sole inheritor. The wagon city had never known any Master but Tycho and then his son. How could it harbor places of which Rombol knew nothing?

Once in the dim hallway, Rombol had no trouble seeing the doors. Setting Byrni down, he moved to the first, trying keys. None seemed to fit the lock. He rattled the brass knob, then passed along the corridor to where it emerged into Lesser Candleway. All the while he muttered under his breath and ran his hands over the walls, peering often at the ceiling or the floor, which Cymbril now noticed was dustier than the Rake's other passages.

No one swept this hallway. No one even knew it was here—no one but Cymbril. The thought made her shiver. *Why can I see it?* she wondered.

Hearing a furtive, flopping sound, Cymbril jumped and glanced toward the end of the hallway, where it opened into Tinley. The warty fat frog sat there, its throat slowly puffing in and out, its moonlike eyes glaring. Rombol hissed at it and waved an arm. Without hurrying, the frog hopped away, its pale legs flashing. It was so ponderous that its ambulation thumped the deck.

"These doors are locked," Rombol said to Cymbril. "How did you get in?"

Cymbril hated to give away her secrets, but she really had no choice. "There are ways to crawl in from above."

"Hmm," he said, scowling. "You and the cats and the rats." He stuck a thick finger in front of her nose. "Go to bed, Cymbril. It won't do to have you headachy and fainting tomorrow. Yellow dress, gold belt and cape. Don't think you're forgiven, and *stay away from the Curdlebrees*."

Clenching her teeth to keep from saying any one of the things she was thinking, Cymbril curtsied and hurried off.

If only Urrt were aboard tonight . . . But her questions for him would have to wait. She could feel weariness overtaking her. Weariness would be worse at first light, when she must struggle out of bed and sing again.

Another grueling day followed, during which she again sang herself hoarse. The crowds never seemed to tire of "The Mountain Brook," with its endless, dizzying *tra-la-la-la-la*s. Cymbril caught one distant glimpse of the Curdlebree twins on their lunch break. They were holding up dresses at a tailor's stall and fighting each other for the chance to admire themselves in a brass mirror. *We're so different,* Cymbril thought.

She glanced down at her own dress, yellow as the morning light, with gold thread here and there that flashed in the sun. In the markets, village girls touched her sleeves, fingered her pleats and capes with longing. But the finery left Cymbril unmoved. She had a trunkful of dresses that a princess might envy—yet she would trade them all for comfortable, durable clothing such as Brigit had worn, the woman who brought Loric to the Rake. Riding garb, world-wandering garb, the raiment of the forest . . . Cymbril thought of lines from the song "The Green Leaves of Eireigh":

A strong bow of yew and boots of good leather,
A kindness of sun, the wind in the heather,
A jerkin of green and a mantle of gray,
And a steed to carry me far and away,
A steed to carry me back to Eireigh.

Under the bright sky, Cymbril thought less about the mysterious corridor and more about Loric, the strange Sidhe boy across the marketplace. How had Brigit captured him? And why, when Cymbril glanced toward him, was he so often gazing back at her? At noon Rombol took Loric indoors and reappeared without him—resting him, Cymbril guessed, for the night road to Corin's Corners.

There were frightening tales of the Sidhe. A merchant had spoken once of glimpsing three Fey astride great gray horses in the moonlight. A scullery maid had told of a Sidhe boy who had wooed her when she was young, long before she came to the Rake. The silver-haired boy, she said, had played a harp outside her window when the stars blazed. She'd been saved only by the holy symbols her father had set on poles around the garden—but she said the word "saved" in a hesitant way and sighed when she finished the story.

All agreed that the Sidhe came among humans in secret, most often at night, and chose certain ones to lead away to their hidden realm. The speakers implied that this abduction was a bad thing, but Cymbril had trouble following their logic. When you were a slave in the world of humankind, wouldn't an "abduction" to a land of dancing be more of a *rescue?*

Cymbril was never one to keep wondering. Curiosity had to be satisfied, just like the stomach when it clamored for food. One way or another, she would have to talk to Loric.

In the late afternoon, the Strongarms filed back from the woods, moving half as slowly as the sun. Urrt sat on a boulder and listened to Cymbril's last few songs. Before he lumbered up the ramp, he obliged the crowd, earning a pocketful of coins by lifting a hay wagon over his head. He crawled beneath it, and when he slowly stood, raising his arms, the wagon seemed at first to be floating upward by itself. For another fee, he repeated the performance—this time with the wagon full of bulky farmers.

Cymbril envied the Armfolk. They were strong and wise; Master Rombol and the crowds respected them and paid them for their work. When some chose to leave the Rake, they went. They were not slaves.

In her years aboard the Rake, Cymbril had made two attempts at escape. The more recent had been at this city's market the previous year. She'd saved a tattered cloak from a pile of worn-out clothes waiting to be cut up for rags. Having gathered food and a threadbare skirt and blouse, she'd tied them up inside the cloak and smuggled the bundle out into the market with a basket of embroidered scarves. In purple dusk, while the merchants packed up, Cymbril had retrieved her bundle from a hollow stump. With great cunning, she'd sneaked into the forest's edge, where an evening mist coiled among the roots. *I'm free!* she'd thought, staring into the dark woods stretching away. She took a step forward, and another, even when she heard the far-off howling of wolves. But then, somewhere much closer, a man's deep voice had laughed harshly. Out among the black trees, a man was laughing, and the tone sounded purely cruel. Her heart suddenly full of chill, Cymbril looked back toward the Rake. On a hill, she'd seen Urrt standing motionless, his round eyes searching the distance as if he knew something was wrong. Cymbril let out a shaky breath and dashed back to slavery, getting to the ramp before the last merchants were inside. No one had been the wiser—except Urrt, perhaps, but he said nothing of it.

As the sun sank among fiery clouds, Rombol swaggered away to a feast with the fur-capped lords of Highcircle. Normally, Cymbril lingered outdoors as long as possible, though she never forgot the evil laughter she'd heard in the forest. She loved to watch twilight fill the hollows, to wait for the first stars to appear. But instead of lingering, she sprang up, determined to take full advantage of the disorganized hour of supper. She could visit the Pushpull Chamber later, but this might be a chance to speak with Loric. She dodged through the jumble of collapsing tents and half-loaded wagons, sprinted up the ramp, and made sure they counted her at the Rake's entrance. Hurrying to the kitchens, she sought out Aubra, a cook who sometimes smiled sadly at her.

"Please, mistress," Cymbril said breathlessly, "does the Sidhe boy come here for supper?"

"'Deed, no," said Aubra, sifting a handful of spice into

a bubbling pot. "The little 'un eats biscuits and a bowl o' cream and touches no meat. Runa takes it to 'im."

"Please, mistress, may I take it to him tonight?"

Aubra smiled, showing dimples, and half lowered her heavy eyelids at Cymbril. "Want a close look at 'im, do you, dear? Well enough—fetch that big tray."

It was not often that Cymbril questioned the wisdom of something she'd already launched into. But as she left the kitchen, her feet stopped, and she stood still in the corridor for a long moment. A thrill of anxiety coursed through her.

He's only a boy, she told herself. *Boys aren't terrifying, and they're never as complicated or dangerous as girls.* Yet this was a boy from beyond the world's edges.

Her palms were sweating as she forced herself to walk onward.

Chapter 6

Loric

Loric was kept in a tiny, windowless storage space with an ironbound door barred on the outside. Cymbril remembered that the room had once been used to confine a pickpocket who had crept aboard the Rake and been caught by Bale the hound. Bale was much less gentle with trespassers than the men-at-arms were. Rombol boasted that the dog's favorite treat was thieves' fingers. In fact, when the pickpocket had been handed over to soldiers in Windwall, both his hands had been wrapped in bandages. Cymbril never passed this place without remembering that glimpse, and the memory did nothing to calm her nerves now as she set the tray on the floor and laid her hands on the timber beam. The other slaves weren't barred into their rooms. There was no need for it; the wilderness was not kind to travelers on foot, and Rombol had friends in every town. But the Master kept Loric behind oak and iron. Was it only because Loric was an expensive investment—or because Rombol was afraid of him?

Loric couldn't be much threat if Runa, a little wisp of a girl, brought him his food. *Just be on your guard,* Cymbril told herself. Taking care to avoid splinters, she slid the beam out of its brackets.

When she pulled open the door, Loric was sitting on his bedroll, his knees bent and ankles crossed. The heavy iron collar was still around his neck, its chain locked to a ring bolted into the wall. His own clothes must be away in the laundry, because he was dressed now in the patched tunic and trousers of the other slaves. The ragged clothes made him shimmer all the more, especially his hair and eyes, like the moon gleaming behind shreds of cloud. Cymbril's own shadow half blocked her view of him. The only light came from a lantern on the corridor wall. As it flickered, Loric's eyes shifted in color, now liquid brown, now golden.

He watched her without speaking. She had the sudden thought that he might be comparing her to Runa, deciding who was prettier. She felt her cheeks beginning to burn, and it annoyed her.

"They haven't given you a lamp," she said.

"I don't need one," answered Loric in that clear, strangely accented voice.

Oh, yes. He could see in the dark, like an owl, like the cats. That idea bothered her, too—the image of him sitting in the lightless room, perfectly calm and vigilant.

Don't gawk, she commanded herself. *Don't be like the market crowds. Hair is hair, and skin is skin. He's just a boy.*

"Cymbril," he said slowly, as if it meant more than her name. "You sing beautifully."

Her forearms tingled. He must have heard her name in the market.

Smiling, he held out his hands for the tray and bowed deeply to her as he accepted it. "You already know my name," he said. "You heard it when the Master bought me."

Cymbril felt her eyes widen. "How did you know I was there?"

"I saw you in the wagon."

"I was hooded."

"You think a hood hides you? Here?" He gave a laugh like the trill of a reed pipe, though something in his gaze convinced Cymbril he was not laughing at her but at the very idea.

She watched him uncover the dishes, the tray laid across his lap. "What do you mean?" she asked.

"Well, you don't belong here, do you? Any more than I do."

He knew, then, that Cymbril wasn't the child of a merchant, like the brats who slapped and kicked and ordered around slaves old enough to be their parents. But she felt the strangest mixing of emotions at his words. She was thrilled to hear someone from outside the Rake say that she didn't belong to it. Yet it was the only home she'd ever had. Loric didn't know her—who was he to decide such things?

Before he ate, Loric crossed his wrists, hands flat against his chest, and murmured something in his own language—a prayer. Then he bit one of the biscuits and studied Cymbril as he chewed. "Would you like some?"

"No, thank you." She knelt in the open doorway. Probably Runa didn't stay and watch him eat. The hall was empty now, but anyone might wander past. There wasn't much time. "Don't the iron chains burn you?" Cymbril crept closer.

A mischievous twinkle came to his eyes. "There are ways of overcoming iron," he said. "Try to guess the secret for yourself."

Cymbril blinked, not sure what to make of his answer. Perhaps she'd have better luck with a different question. "How did Brigit catch you?"

He regarded her and took his time answering, finishing the biscuit first.

Cymbril fidgeted, trying to watch over her shoulder.

"The other girl doesn't ask me questions," he said at last.

"I'm a different girl."

"Yes." Again an irritating pause. "The Lady on the horse caught me because I climbed out through the wall of our world into this one, to see if the stars looked or sounded any different here. I was listening to the stars instead of the forest around me. Quite careless."

Stars—with sounds? "*Are* the stars different here?"

"Not the ones you can see from these lands," he said, picking up the bowl of cream. "But we can see a lot more from Gorhyv Glyn."

Cymbril tipped her head to the side. Gorhyv Glyn. "Is that the Sidhe world?"

"Not all of it. Just the part I'm from." He drank the cream so carefully, it didn't even whiten his upper lip. "Many of the Sidhe—the Dusk Folk—live under the ground now, in deep caverns, ever since the war long ago. My people are the Star Folk. We live in the forests, under the lights of the sky. And Gorhyv Glyn is only one part of the woodland realms. The Sidhe world is very wide, just like the human one."

"You want to go back," Cymbril said, to be sure. She'd learned to take nothing for granted.

"I do, yes."

"Is your family looking for you?"

Once more Loric fell silent.

Cymbril clucked her tongue with impatience. "We haven't got all night, you know. If they find me talking to you, they won't like it."

"Really?" Loric raised his brows. "They don't know you're here?"

"No."

"They didn't send you to bring my supper?"

She started to shake her head but glared at him instead, feeling her throat and cheeks starting to burn again.

"Then why *are* you here?" He looked at her keenly, as if somehow he might see answers whether she spoke them or not.

"Never mind." Cymbril backed away, brushing dust from her skirt. "I'm not here. I'm gone." She glanced at the wooden beam for bolting his door.

"Wait, Cymbril."

He said it so earnestly that she stopped, chin lowered, and watched him.

"I'm sorry to upset you. You *seem* sincere, but I have always been taught that the Second Folk are full of guile. Their words may say one thing and their hands another."

Cymbril frowned, working out his meaning. She put her fists on her hips. "You think I'm asking these questions for Rombol?"

Loric smiled wanly. "I know he is your Master, as he is mine. I know you have many privileges that other slaves do not. And I wonder why one who sings all day is delivering supper."

Cymbril was speechless. It had been bad enough when she thought Loric supposed her to be a merchant's daughter. The truth was that he believed her to be a slave who *spied* for the Master. She wished she'd changed out of the yellow dress with its golden cape and belt—she looked like a bauble, something that belonged on the head of Rombol's cane.

"If Rombol wanted to know your secrets," she said, "he would twist your arms or beat you with a rod until you told him everything." She stepped out through the door. "I'll send Runa after the tray. She's more to your liking—a proper slave who asks no questions."

Cymbril closed the door with a crash. Struggling with the heavy beam, she shoved it through its brackets. A splinter sank into the heel of her hand. With a cry more of ire than pain, she dug the wood sliver out and stamped back to the kitchens.

Privileges.

What gave Loric the right to judge her, this boy without a scar or a callus on his hands, who had the leisure to crawl about in the forest listening to the voices of the stars? Wearing an iron collar for a while might do him some good.

When Rombol's dining party had returned, the Rake rolled again, beginning the overnight journey to Corin's Corners. It was good to sit by Urrt's feet in the Pushpull Chamber and listen to a new song the Urrmsh had woven together during their time in the mossy wood. To Cymbril, though, it sounded exactly like all their other songs—and their tales, for that matter, since she could rarely tell what was spoken and what was sung. Urrt's bench-mate, Arrbha, explained that the makings for this song had come from the birds, who brought news when no local Urrmsh were present. As they sang, some of the Armfolk clicked their toenails in a rhythm on the planks—not for every song, but for this one, which was lively. Those rowers who sat near puddles would sometimes bring down a foot to make a mighty splash.

Having lost so much sleep the night before, Cymbril

had nodded off repeatedly during the singing, her stomach full and her day's energy more than spent. But when Arrbha spoke of birds, Cymbril opened her eyes.

"Isn't it true that the birds talk with the Sidhe?"

"True it is, little thrush," said Urrt. "Birds talk with any who will listen." One of the lanterns just above Urrt's head swung gently, sending his huge, warty shadow to and fro.

Cymbril watched the play of pinkish light and darkness over the glistening boards. "Then couldn't the birds tell Loric's family where he is?"

"Oh, his people know where he is, songbird," Arrbha said. "The birds have never stopped watching where his steps have led."

"Will they come for him, then? His family?" She imagined a host of gray-cloaked riders thundering out of the night, climbing the Rake's sides on silver ropes. Would they do battle with Rombol's soldiers—or would there be negotiations in the ramp chamber, the Sidhe paying a ransom with gold or bright jewels? Cymbril gazed at her stone and hairpin, her heart fluttering. She longed for a chance to see them, the Fey who would come to take Loric home.

But Urrt's answer disappointed her.

"They will not come," said Urrt. "The doors of the Rake

are closed to the Sidhe. There is powerful magic here, of a different sort from theirs."

Cymbril remembered—Brigit had spoken of protective spells upon the wagon city. She took a long breath. So Loric was alone, then, beyond the help of his people.

"Rivers flow and the sky turns," Arrbha said helpfully. "All things in time. These walls are good at keeping things out, but not nearly so good at keeping things in. You needn't worry much about the Fey boy."

"I'm not worried about him," Cymbril said quickly. "He's rather arrogant, if you ask me." To change the subject, she told them what had happened the night before and about the hallway Rombol had never seen before.

"The books in that storeroom are marked with an *R*," she finished, scooting over to avoid a new drip from the ceiling. "I always thought it stood for Rombol, but now I don't think so."

Urrt's bumpy forehead wrinkled, and he conversed with Arrbha in the language of the Urrmsh. At last he turned the full moons of his eyes back to Cymbril. "Nightingale," he said seriously, "in the time of the Rake's first Master, there was a sorcerer onboard. He advised Master Tycho in many ways. They built this place together, and enchantments are twined through every board and nail like the roots of ivy. For a while, the sorcerer had a tower on the aft castle, where the horse barns are now. But it had a way of attracting bolts of lightning—even out of a clear sky. He tore it down and built his quarters deep in the hold, on a secret half-deck."

"None of us knew exactly where," Arrbha said. "We could hear the echoes of pounding and crackling, or a rushing like wind—and sometimes that wild laughter of his—but I never figured out the location."

Cymbril rose to her knees, clutching a pillar leg of the rowing bench as she looked from Urrt to Arrbha.

"That talking skull you showed us," said Arrbha, lowering his voice and checking first to see if Wiltwain was in the chamber—"that was his work. The books would be his, too. I wasn't sorry to see him go. But, truth be told, I'm sorrier now to have those who replaced him."

"His name," said Urrt in a burbly whisper, "was Ranunculus."

Cymbril leaned forward. "What happened to him?"

Urrt shook his head. "No tale of men or song of birds has the answer. We were in the witching country when he disappeared, out at the edge of the Groag Swamp. Some say a spell of his went wrong and consumed him. Some believe he perished in battle with an enemy more terrible than himself.

Or perhaps he simply felt the end of his long life to be near and went into the swamp to find his grave."

Cymbril sat back on her heels, trying to understand. "But why have I always seen that hallway? Why me, and no one else?"

The bench-mates could only shrug. Finally Urrt said, "I think you have very good eyes, skylark."

Chapter 7

The War Goes On

Corin's Corners was no more than a scattering of huts, shops, and a granary around a crossroads. Rombol stopped there mostly because the village was a night's journey from Highcircle, a point halfway to the city of Panoply—and the chance to sell a bag of salt, a copper kettle or two, to the farm wives was better than nothing. So few people lived at the Corners that the Rake's merchants didn't bother to take their wares outdoors. Instead, the ramp was lowered, and the villagers came aboard to a market set up in the grand bailey of the Rake's entrance chamber.

For such indoor markets, Jonas the carpenter had built Cymbril a perch on the second-level balcony, a semicircular projection of the floor with its own ornate railing. She stood there to sing, her voice soaring into the lantern-hung heights above, while vendors and buyers conducted business on the wide floor below. The high place was a welcome change. Here Cymbril was away from those who stared and prodded. A rare customer might be admitted up to the second floor, strictly by arrangement—some traveling noble who wished to be shown the delicate dining sets from the Isles, the silks, tapestries, rugs, and vases that cost more than common folk earned in a year.

The bad part of indoor markets was that the bejeweled ladies from the teabunks tended the extravagant second-level booths. Having nothing to do all day, they gossiped and brewed exotic tea in silver pots. They played horses-and-spindles, a game on a polished board. And always they murmured catty things about Cymbril as if she weren't there listening. Cymbril never felt comfortable turning her back to them, especially not at the balcony rail. Even when she sang, she tried to keep her ears open for the pad of slippers.

Scattered applause followed Cymbril's rendition of "Blue Were Her Eyes." Leaning on the rail to rest and study the crowds, she started at a whispery thump just behind her. She whirled with a gasp. Back in the shadows under the loggia, two ancient women were crossing the balcony, hobbling on their gnarled walking sticks—and hopping just ahead of them was the fat frog, which they treated as a pet. When the frog wasn't lurking in dim corners and staring as if delivering an accusation, he was hurrying as with some purpose. Cymbril wondered if he did errands for the old women.

The crones sold charms and medicines from a tent that always seemed murky, even outdoors at noon. The women—sisters, Cymbril guessed—had three eyes between the two of them, and she could have sworn that the missing eye switched at times from one woman to the other. For that reason, she thought of them as the Eye Women. It was rare to see them outside the gloom of their shop, indoors or out.

Cymbril looked quickly away, but the two had stopped and were gazing at her. One pointed with her stick. They wore scarves of an ugly yellow, the color of dead stalks in autumn. Though they were far away and conversing in their husky voices, Cymbril was sure she heard one of the women say, "She's the one as found it."

A chill spread through Cymbril. *I'm the one? What did I find?* She glanced around, but there was no one else the pair might be talking about. Beyond the rail was only the market bailey itself, one story below.

She felt a wave of dizziness and wiped her clammy forehead on her cuff. As the Eye Women hunched along, vanishing through a shadowy doorway, her head cleared. Probably she'd misinterpreted the words—at that distance, the crone might have muttered anything. "She's the one as found it" made no sense at all. Maybe the woman had been pointing at the cloudy sky outside a window hatch and said, "See, the sun's not out yet."

Just then Wiltwain emerged from a stairwell and turned his steps toward Cymbril.

"Find your lunch," he told her. "Grosnin fed you yesterday? Go to Ubelard at the second baker's stall—see it there? He'll give you lunch today."

Cymbril curtsied and headed for the nearest crank basket, grateful for the break.

Down in the market, she moved quickly. To dally was to invite a circle of curious admirers. Heads turned to watch her, but her brisk pace gave onlookers every reason to suppose she was carrying out some task. She followed the loggia to where Loric sat on a bench, his chain affixed to a pillar. It was horrible to treat anyone this way, she thought as she drew closer, trying to remain unnoticed behind the row of carts and stalls. It bothered her enough when a dog or donkey was kept on a rope. Loric was not human, to be sure—he was of the Wild and perhaps dangerous. But even so, to see him in the heavy collar made her angry.

She couldn't have said why she took herself to the Fey

boy, or why she wanted to see him up close again, or what she had intended to say. Rombol stood at a distance, talking with the commander of the Rake's soldiers. As Cymbril stopped just behind Loric's bench, a woman in a checkered headscarf was tugging her two children away. They went reluctantly, stretching their arms for a last touch of his hair, a final pull on his hand.

Cymbril fingered her sleeve, suddenly nervous. How should she announce her presence? And, for that matter, *why* should she? What was she doing here?

Loric turned half toward her. "I would ask you to come and sit," he said, "but I'm sure our master would not approve."

He'd spoken so casually that Cymbril searched in all directions to be certain he was talking to her. So he'd seen her stalking closer. Wonderful. What a fool she must seem.

"I hope you will forgive me for misspeaking last night," he said.

He was apologizing!

Cymbril thought carefully and said, "I get angry too easily."

"No. It was wrong of me. If I had thought my suspicions through—"

"How old are you?" Cymbril blurted.

He smiled, perhaps surprised. "Thirteen. And yes, we count the years just as you do. Summer, autumn, winter, spring: nature will not be misunderstood, in your world or in mine."

Cymbril could not suppress a grin. He spoke like someone much older. But then again, because she spent so much time with the Armfolk and inside her own head, so did she.

"They are magical, you know." He glanced back at her before looking away again, across the sparse crowd.

"What do you mean? What is?"

"What you have in your pocket."

Startled, Cymbril dropped her hand to her pocket to feel the bulk of her two treasures. "How can you possibly know what I have in my pocket?"

He chuckled. "An ability my people have. I see two beautiful lights shining in your pocket."

Cymbril drew an astonished breath, but just then Rombol noticed her and scowled. "I have to go," she muttered, and hurried on her way.

The cooks and bakers at the markets took turns giving Cymbril her lunch, for such were Master Rombol's orders. Most did so gladly, since her singing helped to draw the crowds, and the crowds brought their appetites. But a few, such as Ubelard, complained to her every single time. "The smiths don't give you horseshoes, I'll warrant." He pinched a roll between his thumb and finger before slapping it onto a tray. Cymbril was sure he always used her as a chance to clear out whatever was going stale.

"Thank you, Master Ubelard," she said cautiously. She carried the tray out through the back of the stall, avoiding the benches in front where the villagers sat to eat. Settling herself on the floor out of sight, she balanced the lunch on her lap. Ubelard had been unusually generous: two rolls, a biscuit, and a pastry with nuts.

The baker leaned out and handed her a tin cup of water. "The silk dyers don't keep you supplied with handkerchiefs, I'll warrant."

"Thank you, Master Ubelard."

No sooner had she taken a bite of the first roll—which was indeed well on its way to becoming a rock—than something heavy landed in her lap with a crash, sending bread and water flying. Cymbril shrieked and flung her arms over her face.

It was a stout chunk of firewood that had struck her. Catching her breath, Cymbril looked up to see Gerta Curdlebree standing over her, cackling and bouncing on her toes.

"Oops!" Gerta said. "One got away from me!" In her arms, she held the rest of a bundle of wood. There were still faint, bluish streaks on her face from the Moonpine dye.

Anger flared in Cymbril, and she sprang to her feet.

Berta appeared on her other side, waggling a finger. "Leave my sister alone, you chicken arms!" She shoved Cymbril back against the wall of the baker's booth.

"Chicken arms!" Gerta taunted, spinning with the load of wood as if it were her dance partner. "Chicken arms!"

"Stop it!" Cymbril said, pushing back at Berta, who didn't seem to realize it was impossible to shove Cymbril farther than the wall.

Cymbril raised her foot, but she stopped herself just short of bringing it down on Berta's mostly healed instep. It seemed too cruel to hurt someone so insufferably stupid. She decided instead to unleash a scream into the girl's ear—but she was still drawing her deep breath when there was a loud *crack!* and Berta fell to her knees, clutching her head.

Ubelard stood in his rear doorway, wielding a heavy stirring spoon. With another lash of his arm, he used the spoon to whack Gerta on the head. Her firewood clattered to the floor. He delivered a second lick to Berta. By this time, both sisters had gotten the idea. Whimpering, they fled as if from a hailstorm, and Ubelard shouted after them that they'd best not prey on the innocent and that they should leave smaller folk alone. "And if your beldam don't like the knots on your noggins, she can take it up with me!"

Cymbril sagged against the wall, rubbing her arms. Berta's grip would probably leave bruises. Her back stung, too.

"Don't mind the bread, girl," said Ubelard gruffly. "I'll fetch you some more." He held up the spoon meaningfully between them. "The men-at-arms: they don't fight for you with their fine swords and pikes, I'll warrant."

Cymbril looked him in the eye. "Thank you, Master Ubelard." In truth, she felt more sorry than thankful. The seamstress had said that the twins were losing their minds. Whatever was wrong with them, it had turned them into bullies. But whacking them on the head or boxing their ears didn't seem like a good treatment—it hardly seemed fair.

The commotion had not escaped Wiltwain's watchful gaze. He soon had the story from Cymbril and from Ubelard. Ordering Cymbril to rest until he returned, he strode away to see the twins and their mother.

Cymbril curled up on a second-floor bench—well away from the teabunk ladies—and closed her eyes. She'd seen Loric watching her as she recrossed the market floor. All she could feel for the Curdlebree twins was pity. Their ridiculous hatred for her was like a poisonous weed that Cymbril was determined to uproot and toss into a fire. Problems such as this couldn't be left unfixed. The solution wasn't revenge. It was finding some way to help the sisters.

"'Chicken arms'?" she repeated to herself, critically examining her own skinny arms and wondering if, in the clouded world of Berta's and Gerta's minds, chickens had arms.

Once, in the dusty soil at the end of a market day, Cymbril had found a child's bracelet of glass beads. She'd shown it to Wiltwain, who told her to keep it. Now, having been lying in wait for Runa outside the kitchens, Cymbril offered it to the dark-eyed girl in exchange for the chance to carry Loric's tray to him—and, more importantly, for Runa's promise of silence.

"It's ugly," Runa said, holding the bracelet up to a lamp. But she stuffed it into her skirt pocket and handed over the tray.

At Loric's room, before she'd even greeted him, Cymbril launched into her question: "What do you mean my treasures are magical?" Of course they were enchanted to glow as they did. But she hoped he could tell her more.

Loric's eyes twinkled. "If you will lend me the smaller one, I'll show you."

She hesitated, still unnerved by the fact that he could see

the treasures inside her pocket. She'd never given the hairpin to another person, even to hold. But what harm could there be? Loric was chained to the wall. Slowly, she drew the pin out and placed it into his palm.

"It's exquisite," he said. Then, with a mysterious wink, he held it up between them, turning it between his thumb and middle finger. The light of the stone brightened, and Cymbril held her breath.

Lowering it, Loric touched the pronged end to the center of his tray. Cymbril covered her mouth as the three biscuits slid across the wood, moving by themselves. When they bumped to a stop against the pin's shank, Loric wiggled the fingers of his other hand. The firelit stone flashed in response, and the biscuits slid away again, each moving to a different corner of the tray. One circled the cream bowl on its way.

Then the cream rose in tendrils, stretching out of the bowl, following Loric's free hand. It stood on end like a tower of white clouds, leaving most of the bowl empty, until he let it settle again—and it was once more a rippling liquid.

Cymbril clapped her hands in wonder and took the pin back, trying the tricks herself. But nothing she did made the stone glow any brighter. The biscuits didn't move, and the cream stayed in the bowl.

"It takes time and practice," Loric said. "My mother would scold me for playing with food."

While he ate and drank, Cymbril found herself telling him the story of what had happened behind Ubelard's. Then, in response to his polite urging, she recounted everything that had passed between her and the two sisters. Only on this telling, she was also honest about what had prompted her to scream at Hysthia Giltfeather.

Loric smiled, his lustrous brown eyes searching her eyes. She looked away with a fire in her cheeks and neck that was becoming familiar lately.

"My parents," he said, "teach that compassion can do much to unravel the tangles of life. And this is a tangled knot."

"But I tried," Cymbril said, "with Byrni—"

"You tried to show kindness," Loric answered, "but it was misunderstood. Perhaps if you try again, more carefully—if we look for a way together . . ."

Cymbril hung her head, thinking.

"What's wrong?" he asked, resting his chin in his palms.

She massaged her arms, which had developed a dull ache from Berta's attack. *Why do I keep wanting to talk to you?* she wondered. *Why do I think of you all the time?* Aloud, she asked, "Am I under a Fey spell?"

He laughed softly. "Now it would be *my* turn to go away angry, if I were not chained to the wall."

Cymbril cocked her head.

Loric continued. "You're suspicious of me, aren't you? You've been taught that the Fey kidnap humans."

"Don't they, ever?"

He shrugged. "The Dusk Folk might. I know from experience that humans capture Fey. But think about it: if I had put you under a spell, you would be dancing with your head full of moonlight and pale flowers—not worrying whether you were under a spell."

She watched him slyly.

"Now," he said, leaning forward, "can you tell me what Gerta and Berta want the most? What do *they* think would make them happy?"

Cymbril didn't have to think for long. "They want to be beautiful. They're always fussing over their hair, and they can't pass a mirror without stopping."

"Is that all?" Loric seemed to gaze far away, deep in thought. "Then I think I know a way."

Cymbril regarded Loric carefully. In her years on the Rake, she'd seen the ways of hard-driving merchants, how they treated one another and people in general. "Why are you so eager to help me?" she asked.

He gazed back strangely, as if puzzled by the question. "Isn't that what people do—help each other? We're all part of one another."

"From what I've seen, most people don't help others unless there's payment involved or they're forced to," Cymbril said.

"You're making me shiver," said Loric. "This world is cold, this place of few stars. But here's an answer that may meet with your approval. I'll help you, and at the same time, you can do something to help me."

Cymbril shrugged. "Go on."

Loric pushed up his right sleeve to the elbow and held his slender arm in the air. "What do you see here?" he asked.

Cymbril frowned. Was this a magic trick? Listening for any approach in the corridor, she said impatiently, "Five fingers, including a thumb. What am I supposed to see?"

He smiled and pointed to his bare arm near the wrist. "Look here."

Cymbril drew a surprised breath. Strapped to Loric's arm was a tiny cloth bag. How had she missed seeing it? But when she moved her gaze by a fraction, his arm looked completely bare again. The bag only became visible when she stared directly at it.

"This is a symbol of diverting," Loric explained, indicating a complex glyph stitched onto the bag with silver thread. "It's kept my coin purse secret since I was captured." He unbound the cords and held the bag out to Cymbril.

She took it cautiously. It was too light to be filled with much of anything. She reached for the drawstring.

"I wouldn't waste time counting the coins now," Loric said. "I think you'll have just enough, although you'd have more if the moon were fuller. Still, it can't be helped. You have to do your buying when the Night Market is open."

"What?"

"A Night Market is going to be held—here, in this rolling city, on the fourth night from now. You'll have to wait till then."

Cymbril shook her head. "What are you talking about? How can you possibly know anything about the Rake and what happens here?"

Loric grinned. "Your friend Miwa is a talkative cat and quite helpful. She told me about the Night Market. If we're lucky, they'll have what we need. I'll tell you exactly how to get in and what to buy."

Cymbril watched him closely, holding back her questions. "I'm listening," she said.

Chapter 8

The Dark Door on the Right

Though she'd always confided everything to Urrt, for some reason Cymbril didn't feel like telling him about her complicated feelings toward Loric. They seemed intensely private, and she didn't understand them herself. When she thought of Loric, there was a thrill behind her ribs. But there was a sense of danger, too. She said nothing to the Urrmsh of the plans she and Loric had made concerning the Night Market. Urrt would certainly warn her against it, and she didn't want to act against his wishes.

To take her mind off Loric, she told Urrt about her encounter with the Eye Women and what she thought she'd heard one of them say.

Urrt shook his bulbous head. "Those ladies are friends

of no one, songbird. You would do well to stay as far from them as sunrise is from sunset."

Cymbril nodded agreement. "Why does Master Rombol allow them on the Rake—them and their awful frog?"

Pondering the question, Urrt worked the oar, rocking steadily forward and back in the lamplight. His present bench-mate was Bembhaa, who had never learned more than a few words of human speech. Whenever Cymbril spoke to him, Bembhaa rumbled with quiet laughter that made his huge belly shake. Then he would pat her head and answer in a purr-ing stream of Urrmsh words.

"I told you of the old sorcerer, Ranunculus," Urrt said at last. "Not long after he vanished, those two ladies—sisters, they are—came to Master Tycho with proof that they were cousins to Ranunculus and his only living heirs. They de-manded his place aboard the Rake."

"So they advise Master Rombol?" Cymbril asked.

"I think not, little thrush. When his father died, Master Rombol left things as they were, but I've never seen him speak to the ladies at all. Near as I can tell, he stays out of their way, and they keep to themselves."

"I wonder why they want to be here," said Cymbril.

"Best not to wonder about them at all, little linnet," said Urrt.

Bembhaa chortled suddenly, patting Cymbril's head, and merrily repeated words he didn't understand, forming them with effort: "At all, little linnet. At all, little linnet."

The next four days crept by in cycles of work, sleep, and the songs of the Urrmsh. There was a grand two-day market in Panoply, complete with a joust put on by the Knights Fountainers, which gave Cymbril an afternoon's rest from singing. She was allowed to watch, but she found no amusement in the brutal sport. The knights were good and brave men, sworn to protect the weak, and for such work, they must be warriors. But a joust was more frightening than exciting, with the pounding hooves, the crash of padded lances on shields, the rough unseating of knights. Always at such events, some were injured, limping or carried off the field. Why did the crowds cheer at such things? Loric was right: the world of the Second Folk was cold and cruel.

Cymbril pondered what Loric had told her. He could talk to the Rake's cats, or so he claimed. True enough, they seemed to like him. When Rombol displayed Loric in the markets, there was often a cat curled contentedly at the boy's feet. The fat frog, on the other hand, glowered at him from beneath wagons. The frog's dislike, Cymbril thought, was a definite point in Loric's favor. Then again, the frog seemed to disapprove of everyone.

The purse contained seven coins of a surprisingly light weight, each about half the size of Cymbril's palm. By day they were a dull bronze color, without markings of any kind. At night a little over half of each coin's surface glowed with a brilliant hue, just like the waning gibbous moon in the sky. From certain angles, Cymbril could glimpse a face in each bright swath—a face turned mostly away from the full to a profile, the Man in the Moon, with merry-looking eyes and a cunning smile.

On the second night after receiving the purse, she had a fright, thinking she'd lost it. She was certain she'd put it into the trunk with her clothing and the two treasures, but it was nowhere to be found. As her panic mounted, she suddenly remembered the symbol of diverting. "It's here," she told herself. "I just can't see it." Moving slowly, she shook out each garment until she heard a small thump and saw an indentation in the hem of her folded red dress. Sure enough, when she looked right at the spot, the coin purse was there.

Eventually, curiosity got the best of Cymbril. She showed one of the coins to Urrt, just to hear what he'd say.

"A moonmarket coin," he rumbled, pushing and drawing the mighty oar. "Did the Fey lad give it to you, little thrush? Most of the Elder folk use them, the Sidhe and—the others."

"So I can't spend it at a market?" She was being devious, curious whether he'd mention the Night Market himself.

Urrt pursed his lips, and his bench-mate looked uneasy. "I wouldn't show it to anyone, songbird. It will only bring trouble to you and the young lad. Put it away, and keep it safe. You know its value changes with the moon? When the moon is full, you'll be richer."

Cymbril scowled. "That's a nonsensical system of money," she said.

Urrt laughed softly. "Indeed? But there are times to buy finer things, and times to buy lesser. A moonmarket coin serves at either time. Isn't that better than a little copper piece that will never amount to much, or a stack of gold when all one wants to buy is a sack of potatoes?"

"The world has no constant values," chimed in the bench-mate, whose name Cymbril didn't know for sure. "The selfsame leaves are green in the summer and golden in the fall. What is fixed about a river—or the sky?"

Early on the third evening, Cymbril took a turn down her once-secret hallway off Tinley to see what Rombol had done about the storerooms. The Master's *X* was still scratched into the floor at the corridor's mouth, and the dull padlocks on the doors had been replaced with shiny new ones. The old, she supposed, had been cut off, since Rombol didn't have keys to them. From the hatchways above, she saw that the rooms had been mostly emptied out. It gave her a lonely feeling that Byrni and his box were no longer on the table. *And whose fault is that?* she reminded herself.

Next came a market day at Brindle and then one at Harn's Ford, where the Rake stopped on a broad stony island in the middle of the shallow Wander River. The booths and tents came down during a glorious sunset, when all the sky was full of red fire and purple shadow, and fireflies winked as cool sparks under the trees.

As Cymbril ate a supper of brown bread, sausages, beans, and cheese, the Rake rolled eastward, splashing through the Wander and up a rocky ravine, the trunks of dead trees snapping beneath the wheels. Cymbril rested as best she could, but she was too excited to sleep. Dressed in a drab brown skirt and a frayed blouse the color of lilacs, she curled on her bed and studied her stone and hairpin.

She would have to leave the treasures here. "Don't take any valuables to the Night Market," Loric had said, "even if you're certain they can't be stolen. Don't take along anything you're not ready to part with."

Night Markets, Loric explained, were held in various places secret to all but a few, and they were moved frequently, because much of what was sold did not exactly belong to the sellers. The Rake provided the perfect venue for a Night Market since it moved all the time.

"It sounds like it's breaking the law," Cymbril said.

Loric nodded. "There are no laws in your King's books to cover what goes on at a Night Market."

"But you're sending me there?" she asked.

"It's not really dangerous," he said, "as long as you don't touch anything you're not buying."

Cymbril didn't have to ask why this was so. Daytime merchants were protective enough of their wares. She supposed those running a Night Market would be all the more suspicious. She eyed Loric doubtfully. "Have you been to one of these?"

"No. But my brother has, and he's told me all about them."

She left her room when the night was deepest and descended quickly, using an out-of-the-way crank basket. On the Rake's second level, she took the darkest side routes toward the aft right quarter of the rolling city. As she neared her destination, Miwa appeared from behind a row of lidded baskets.

Cymbril could only just recognize the cat in the faint glow of the torchmoss growing in clumps on the wall. Miwa purred and circled her feet. The cat always seemed to find her when Cymbril was about to do something risky.

"So you've been talking to Loric," Cymbril whispered, lifting Miwa in her arms. "I wish you could talk to me."

Miwa reached up a paw and batted affectionately at Cymbril's face.

She put Miwa down. The cat pattered just ahead of her, a pale ghost shape in the gloom, her tail held high. "I'll follow you, then," Cymbril murmured.

Cymbril almost never came to this part of the Rake. It was dark in a way she couldn't quite explain and didn't like—a darkness that had nothing to do with the scarcity of lamps. There seemed to be more spider webs in the door frames and among the bracing beams overhead. The floors were unswept, and the timbers of the walls had a dank, unhealthy smell. The maidservants circulated rumors that Rombol kept fierce fighting dogs (or maybe they were wolves) in cages somewhere nearby. Ahead, the passageway of Inbrace dead-ended in a kind of cramped court two stories high.

To Cymbril, it seemed a court by default, its walls formed by the back walls of other structures and levels. Over long years and many reconstructions, these buildings had almost grown together. It was like a cavern in the city's innards, an imperfectly stitched seam in the dark. She edged warily into the strange mildewy place.

At the center of the court was a grotesque statue Cymbril hated. She'd seen it before only from the entrance arch and had been disinclined to approach any closer. It was made of some black pitted wood and represented two battling giants. Clawing and throttling, the two giants were draped with spider webs. Torchmoss tufts higher up cast a faint, cold glow over the warriors, the shadows making their faces more horrible and savage. In the webs, Cymbril saw the many tiny dangling, jiggling bodies of the weavers.

But there was something more ominous than the statue. Across the court, farthest from the lamplight of Inbrace, stood two ironbound doors. The one on the left, Cymbril knew, was the residence of the Eye Women. In the door's lowest quarter was a hinged hatchway that must be for the use of the fat frog.

A single candle burned in an iron fixture between the two doors.

The door on the right—

Truth be told, Cymbril had not noticed this second door

before. Probably her view had been blocked by the statue. This portal looked the same as the other but without the frog hatch.

In the door's center, a placard hung from a spike. Letters were burned into the board in a neat script. They said:

Night Market

Now Open

Purchase or Perish

Enter at Your Peril

Not Responsible

Knock First

By long habit, Cymbril thrust her hand into her pocket to touch the reassuring shapes of the stone and hairpin. Neither, of course, was there. She took a deep breath, trying to ignore the unpleasant odor of the place, and crossed to the Night Market door, giving the statue a wide berth.

As she moved lightly over the moldy, water-swollen

timbers of the floor, she half expected the Eye Women to fling open their doorway or the frog to burst forth. But the only sound was the tread of her leather soles. Maybe the gloom of the place brought a clarity to her thoughts—because all at once she understood what the crone had meant by "She's the one as found it." The hallway. The magical hallway that no one else but Cymbril had been able to find. Of course, the old women were witches. Cymbril was certain of that. They were cousins to Ranunculus, the sorcerer. They must have moved aboard the Rake because they wanted what was in his storerooms! Was it possible they hadn't found those rooms in all the years? And what did it mean that Cymbril had found them and revealed the discovery?

A memory sprang into her mind like a touch of ice. The fat frog had been watching when she'd led Rombol to those secret rooms. She recalled Rombol shooing it away with a hiss. If the frog was a servant to the Eye Women—if it reported to them—then they knew where those storerooms were.

She trembled, but there was no time to worry about such questions at the moment. Lips clamped firmly, she raised a fist to the Night Market door and rapped three times.

A lock turned and the door swung inward, creaking. Hardly daring to breathe, Cymbril took a step forward to the threshold.

Beyond the door a wooden stairway plunged beneath cobwebs and through darkness to what seemed a large fire-lit space four or five stories down. It was impossible. The Rake had only one level below this one. The place at the stairway's foot, if it existed at the distance it appeared to, would be under the ground. The stair did not run straight, but twisted slightly from side to side, the steps all angled differently, their intervals irregular.

Cymbril pressed her hands to her face. Chill sweat seeped onto her skin, and she shrank back, suddenly lightheaded. If all she'd stood to gain was peace with the Curdlebrees, she would have turned right around and gone back to her bunk. But her purpose was to help Loric, too.

It's not really dangerous, he'd said.

Just another market, she told herself. *I have money for it and things to buy. Since when is a paying customer unwelcome?* And besides, if she gave up now, it would be only her fear that had stood in the way of success.

Swallowing on a dry throat, she advanced again.

As she set foot on the top step, two hands shot out of the blackness to her left, fingers raised as if to bar her way—two hands with long claws, the skin a hideous blue-white.

Cymbril shrieked, leaping backwards.

The hands spread themselves as if in exasperation, flapping their voluminous sleeves. The gesture asked her: *Are you coming in or not?*

Gasping for breath, she tried to see who might own the hands. But in the alcove past the door frame, there was only the dark. Unless perhaps, barely visible, two points of light glittered. Eyes.

She clutched her collar and approached again.

The hands rose preventively once more, and now a low, harsh voice spoke:

"By whose invitation?"

Cymbril froze, hovering on the edge of flight, but she remembered Loric's instructions. To get in, she had to mention the names of the Eye Women, who had organized the Night Market. Miwa had told Loric their names.

Cymbril glanced down. Miwa was sitting resolutely beside her, tail twitching as she faced the doorkeeper.

Cymbril cleared her throat. "My hostesses are Mistress Atymnia and Mistress Fennella."

Now one hand turned palm-up and extended itself toward her. When she eyed it in repulsed confusion, the voice said, "Admission fee."

Cymbril had heard nothing of this and didn't like it, but she saw no choice. With her left hand, she undid the drawstring of the purse that, as Loric had done, she'd bound to her right forearm. She eased out one coin, whose half glowed fiercely, the rest of the disc featureless and black. She closed the purse, held her hand well above the doorkeeper's, and dropped the coin.

The yellowish claws closed around the money, curling up like the legs of a dead spider, and the hands dropped away. Cymbril could no longer see the pair of eyes, if she'd seen them at all. The darkness on the stairway was complete.

With a meaningful rub against Cymbril, Miwa scampered ahead.

Magical or not, this is a part of the Rake, Cymbril thought. *And it looks as if I'm not going alone.*

Right hand out to find the wall, she climbed downward.

Chapter 9
The Night Market

Cymbril felt for each step with her toes, the boards squeaking beneath her slippers. Behind, the door closed with a bang. She disliked being in the blackness with the doorkeeper, so she descended quickly toward the firelight. When her hand touched a sticky web, she stifled a cry. Once, she heard Miwa spit angrily and growl at something unseen. Cymbril stood still, heart pounding, as something wheezy and foul-smelling brushed past the hem of her skirt, soft feet making squishing noises. Where the smallish thing might be going, she couldn't imagine.

The light grew. Miwa waited for her at the stairway's foot, where a fire in a tripod brazier threw its glow across the plank floor. The babble of many voices filled the air, along with swirls of laughter and the music of pipes. Cymbril held her breath and peered out past an archway covered with vines and ruby-red berries.

Smoke drifted everywhere, rising from other braziers, from tents lit up by colored fires inside, from bubbling kettles, and from torches whose brackets were shaped into metal birds and gargoyles. A shadowy crowd browsed and chattered. Cymbril hung back, realizing that most of the Night Marketgoers were not human. There were tall folk with dark skin and blue or silver hair. There were men with the legs and horns of goats, women with the transparent wings of moths, and hulking people who seemed formed of moss and stone. Some of the company hid themselves in hoods and cloaks. Others—heads no higher than Cymbril's waist—darted and chased one another among the stalls.

Creatures of the forest were here, too: foxes, wolves with amber eyes, and a bear who rose to his hind legs to search for something, his head above the crowd. These animals moved with dignity and refinement, and no one seemed alarmed at their presence. A wolf put its paws onto a countertop, and Cymbril was certain it spoke with the shopkeeper. She wondered if these were really animals at all or perhaps enchanted folk in disguise.

What baffled her was how the place could be a combination of a huge chamber and a forest glade. There was a deck under her feet, a ceiling above, just like elsewhere on the Rake. But trees stood everywhere, the planks fitting snugly around their trunks. Lanterns hung from the branches. And in the distance on one side, Cymbril could see stars in the night sky. The warm air was alive with spice.

Since nearly everyone who passed stared directly at her, Cymbril decided it was pointless to hide behind the viny arch. Brushing cobwebs from her sleeves, she stepped out into the crowd. She had no idea which direction to go, but it seemed that Miwa did. The cat set off at once through the feet of the marketers, glancing back often to be sure Cymbril was following.

"Walker in daylight!" someone said brightly, and Cymbril looked up to see a thin man in red velvet, his face concealed by an expressionless white mask. He rubbed his palms together, tapping Cymbril often on the shoulder. "Child of the sun! Come and see! Come and see! Wonders and fancies, bargain rates!" He swirled his hands, pointing toward a stall that glowed invitingly with pink light, where necklaces and jeweled belts hung from a rod.

Miwa made an ominous warning sound, the fur standing

up on her back. Cymbril remembered something else Loric had told her: "Don't talk to strangers more than is necessary, don't linger, and don't be distracted from your purpose."

Cymbril gave the briefest of curtsies and dashed off after Miwa.

Through gaps between stalls, she had glimpses of treetops drifting past. The Rake was still rolling, and she was looking out from about the second-story level. This place defied all the natural laws of distance and proportion. Even as she wondered how the marketgoers were able to board the moving wagon city, a crank basket rose through a well in the floor, and out stepped two hedgehogs and an old man with white hair and a beard, his cap and cloak made all of interwoven briars.

Miwa pattered back to rub impatiently against Cymbril's leg. She hurried on after the cat, past a short, swarthy woman juggling lighted candles, each burning with a different-colored flame. As they twirled through the air, the candles hurled globs of hot wax that left smoke trails and splattered among the crowd, making them shriek.

Miwa stopped before a stall whose front counter was draped in purple cloth. Dozens of ornate wire cages lined the counter and hung from interior hooks and from tree limbs above the tent. Inside all the cages were clusters of ripe fruit—apples, golden pears, grapes, plums, peaches, and berries.

The stoop-shouldered man tending the booth had curling ocean waves tattooed on his cheeks and bulbous forehead, like the sailors at Whaleroad. A gold earring flashed as he leaned on his elbows and showed Cymbril a grin of several missing teeth.

Cymbril hesitated, seriously doubting this was the stall she wanted. But Miwa turned back and forth, rubbing along the counter's base, purring and blinking up at Cymbril.

"C'mon, then, little miss!" said the merchant in a voice that sounded as if it had been yelling for too many years. "Ye in the market f'r some caged fruit? Aaaall fresh. Aaaall rripe. Plucked and tucked today. Three f'r the price, two f'r the price, take yer pick, pick yer take."

Cymbril stepped cautiously forward. In a small voice, she asked, "Why is it in cages?"

"Ha-ha-ha!" laughed the booth tender, and she saw with a chill that his tongue was forked at the end, the tongue of a serpent.

"Bee-cause," he said, "it ain't the sort o' fruit we'd want lyin' loose, missy." He winked with one eye, then the other, and wiggled his ears, apparently for Cymbril's entertainment.

"Did ye lose yer mammy and pap? Do they know ye're nosin' 'round the caged fruit stand?"

"Yes, I lost them," said Cymbril, covering her coin purse with her other hand. "They're dead."

"Aahhh," said the merchant. "Well, then, ye've the right to go where ye will—whadda ye say? Aaall fresh. Aaall rripe. Take yer pick, pick yer take."

"Do you sell Nixielixir?" asked Cymbril.

The man stopped his pitch. "And what would ye be needin' that for?"

"Do you sell it?"

He pushed out his lower lip. "I c'd say aye, but I'd be lyin' through me teeth." And he showed his teeth again, such as they were.

Cymbril started to turn away but remembered the other thing she'd come to buy. "And what about skeleton keys?"

Watching her seriously, the merchant wiggled his eyebrows and made his close-shaved scalp slide forwards and backwards on his head. Just when she thought he was ignoring the question, he hooked a thumb over his shoulder. "'Round the back."

She thanked him and circled the booth, staying well away from the cages dangling from low branches. Even so, she thought she saw a pear inside one cage jiggle slightly as she passed, its golden skin pressed to the bars. And did she glimpse a plum swell the tiniest bit, as if it had taken a breath? For the first time, she noticed that the stall had carved dragon claws at the bases of its corner posts, the knuckles and wrinkles lovingly crafted, the talons clutching the roots of trees on either side. Miwa's furry face poked around the booth's edge, seeming to demand, *What's taking you so long?*

In the greenish glare of a low-slung lantern, Cymbril saw that the booth had a rear counter much like the one in front, only narrower and with no caged fruit. It faced another avenue of the Night Market, where a baker's booth sold stacked cakes that smelled wonderful. Next door, four identical black-bearded smiths were nailing horseshoes onto the hooves of a horse that hung suspended in the air by broad leather straps and munched contentedly from a feedbag.

As Cymbril approached the rear counter, she heard a voice from inside the booth, jabbering nonstop. A familiar voice . . .

Byrni!

"Thence, the road leads for three leagues through a dry and slightly rising country to the village of Merl, its fourteen cottages occupied by the families of Blukin, Arble, Pall, Simsop, Lubbinhal . . ."

Cymbril peered into the stall, and again she stared.

Byrni, once a mere skull confined to a wooden box, was now perched atop a "body" that appeared to have been pieced together for him from whatever might be found. His trunk was a dressmaker's dummy, clearly female. Mismatched rods with mismatched hinge joints formed his arms and legs. One hand was a gardener's three-pronged rake, the other a stuffed leather gauntlet. For feet, he had one boot and one scrub brush, both of which stomped the floor in jerky rhythm as he sat balanced in a chair.

"Wainwright, Arndale," he continued, listing the families of Merl, his head rocking and tipping. "Balbery, Venter, Smith, Smith (the second the son of the first) . . ." He seemed to be thoroughly enjoying his new-gained ability to gesture, his arms flailing expressively, threatening the wire fastenings that held him together.

Cymbril saw that two more skeletons occupied two other chairs inside the booth. These were proper human skeletons, all of bones from head to foot. Like Byrni, they could also move. One spread its arms in welcome. The other rose to its feet and bowed, then flourished its hands to display the rows of items for sale.

The skeletons were selling the oddest things: stone jars bore the labels "MUD," "SLIME," "MOLD," "DUST," and "LINT." A smaller fancy jar with handles was labeled "FINE LINT."

Strings bore hundreds of feathers, some beautiful and patterned with rainbow colors, some pathetic and bedraggled. Open trays held thousands of buttons of every shape and color imaginable. There were boxes of glass beads, half-burned candlesticks, pins and brooches, and a few ancient books. Much of the merchandise looked like things that had fallen through the cracks of the world and gotten lost—behind bookshelves, under stairways, beneath floorboards, or in the weedy corners of gardens.

On a shelf lay the velvet cushion, Cymbril noticed, from Byrni's box. And on the cushion curled the skeleton of a small animal, probably a cat. As Cymbril watched, the little skull yawned, and the skeleton stretched itself, kneading the cushion with bony paws before curling up again in a new position.

"Good evening," Cymbril said, feeling less nervous around the skeletons than with the fork-tongued merchant in front. Perhaps it was because Byrni was present—though why that should relieve her, she couldn't imagine. "Good evening, Byrni."

She quickly realized Byrni was the only one who could talk. Certainly he talked more than enough for the three of them. The other two bowed politely at her greeting.

"Ah, it's you!" said Byrni, interrupting himself. "Good to see you, good to see you! Now, where was I? Oh, yes—the cottage of the Blukins is divided into three rooms, two of which have one window apiece . . ."

Cymbril thought the skeleton sitting next to Byrni looked bored.

The one who had risen worked hard to pique Cymbril's interest in different things. It waved its hands impressively to indicate a plate of hard dry objects like pebbles. Peering closer, she saw they were peach pits. The skeleton plunked onto the counter a wire basket of bottles labeled "POND WATER," "SEA WATER," "PUDDLE WATER," "PURE RAIN," "HONEST SWEAT," "TEARS OF PAIN," and "TEARS OF JOY." The skeleton somehow balanced along one arm a rumpled hat, a doll made of nuts and husks, a gilt-framed mirror, a cracked cup, and a slipper. It deposited everything into a heap and brandished in quick, hopeful succession a soup ladle, a cow's horn, a seashell, a tarnished trumpet, a silver box, a dried starfish, and a pinecone. Finally, it thrust into Cymbril's hands a small leather-bound book.

Book of Rejected Words read the gold-etched title on the cover.

Curious, she leafed through the book and saw that all the pages were covered with words in various styles and scripts, some half-finished, most viciously struck through with slashes or X's. She found "sheveled" and "waige" and

"brung" and "dinder" and "insofaras." There were "bewhich,"
"boughten," "fishish," "lilacity," "sternable," "predoubtable,"
"thrice-bepawed," and "interlying." Sideways down the edge
of one page, in flowery calligraphy with purple ink, someone
had written: "peri—pera—para—paira—" followed by a rude
expletive.

Cymbril flipped to the back. The second-to-last page had
just the two words "Forgive me"—and the very last page said
only "I love you."

She closed the sad book and pushed it back across the
countertop. Speaking clearly so as to be heard over Byrni, she
asked, "Do you have skeleton keys, please?"

The shop-keeping skeleton flung up its hands in appar-
ent delight and reached toward the ceiling. From behind a
fringe of velvet curtain, it pulled down a taut cord that was
tied across the booth's interior, like a clothesline. Clipped to
the cord were hundreds and hundreds of keys.

Now the other skeleton—the bored one—hopped up
and helped with the flourishing and bowing.

"Excuse me!" said Byrni as one of the skeletons jostled
him. "The third rafter from the east end in the Arbles' loft is
severely rotted and will need replacing before next spring to
avoid dire consequences."

Cymbril peered in dismay at the enormous selection.

She had hoped "skeleton key" referred to one precise thing. Her only hope, then, was to explain what she wanted it for.

"I need a key that will open a magical iron neck collar. A manacle. It's owned by Master Rombol, if that helps."

The second skeleton clapped and pranced in triumph. The first promptly unclipped a key and smacked it decisively onto the counter.

Cymbril blinked. Could it really be that easy?

As if sensing her doubt, the skeleton ducked behind the counter and came up with an iron collar that looked exactly like the one Loric wore, padlocked just the same. He thrust the key into the lock, turned it with a smart click, and the lock sprang open.

Cymbril glanced down at Miwa, who purred.

The skeleton held up two fingers.

"All right," Cymbril said. She drew two coins from her purse as the skeleton nestled the key into a key-size box of delicate wood and tied it up with red twine. It amazed Cymbril how dexterous the sharp, dry finger bones could be.

Cymbril slid her half-moons across the countertop, thanked the skeletons, and called a farewell to Byrni.

"Farewell until we meet again," he said, waving his gauntlet, and went right on with his sentence: "—which collects in a barrel at the southeast corner of the cottage."

Cymbril was turning to go when the skeleton plucked at her sleeve and dropped into her hand five golden stars, each fashioned with eight pointed rays and no bigger than her thumbnail. She gazed at them in perplexed wonder until she understood that this was her change. She'd paid with two moons and gotten back five stars.

I'll bet these *have a constant value,* she thought. But then she noticed that the stars were twinkling, now brighter, now dimmer. She wondered if they'd vanish altogether on cloudy nights.

Smiling, she thanked the skeletons again and put the stars into her coin purse.

She felt happy and excited to have achieved success so far. But now Miwa trotted ahead hastily, and Cymbril had trouble keeping up. The crowd had thickened, and people bumped and brushed against her. Wary of pickpockets, she kept the key box clutched in her right fist and her left hand covering the purse on her wrist.

For the entertainment of the crowd, a man in a green-and-red suit stood on one hand, upside down atop a long pole. The bells on his pointed hat jingled as he kicked his feet in the air.

They don't have a singer, Cymbril thought with satisfaction and a pang of wistfulness. Part of her felt it would be far more interesting to be the Nightingale of the Night Market. But a cage was a cage. She squeezed the box in her hand.

At the foot of a tree where candles glowed from niches in the bark, four people wearing cloaks and wide-brimmed hats squatted around a heap of moonmarket coins, dividing the money. One of the figures, a woman with rings in her ears and nose, glared up suspiciously. Hurrying onward, Cymbril thought the Night Market was no different in its essence from the daytime ones: buying and selling, and everything had a price. This one only seemed more attractive at first because she was a buyer, not a slave. When she ran out of coins, she would be worse off here than in her daily life. Here she didn't know the rules.

They rounded the end of a row of stalls, and Cymbril stopped with a gasp.

She was face-to-face with Brigit.

Wearing a green hooded cloak, leather breeches, and muddy boots, Brigit looked exactly as she had on the night she brought Loric to the Rake. Her gaze fixed itself on Cymbril, and a strange look of recognition crossed the woman's scarred, beautiful face. Slowly, Wildhair's messenger smiled. "Cymbril," she said.

Miwa spat violently and practically flew to the high limb of a tree, where she clung flat and growling.

Cymbril saw that at least ten of the cowled riders accompanied Brigit, though they were all on foot now. Gripping handles of looped rope, the men were pulling a box on wheels. It was as large as a carriage, though it had no door, windows, or driver's seat, and it was wrapped around and around with ropes, chains, and iron bands.

Stepping close, Brigit reached out with a gloved hand and touched Cymbril's face. "You've grown," Brigit said. Something flickered in her eyes, and she laughed once, through her nose.

Then she ruffled Cymbril's hair, and, keeping a hand on her sword hilt, she led her men onward.

Cymbril stumbled back out of their way, retreating against the tree trunk, and watched as they took the giant box deeper into the market. They were coming in with it, not going out. *She's brought us something else,* Cymbril thought.

And she knows me.

She stood still until the procession was lost among the crowd. When Miwa climbed down from the tree, Cymbril smoothed the cat's fur back into place. "You look like a puffer fish," Cymbril told her.

Miwa led the way again, turning left, then right, then left again past a tent that flashed brilliantly, as if lightning were striking inside it, over and over. Ahead, Cymbril saw the viny arch, its berries shining in the torch light. Miwa had led her back to the stairway. The cat waited on the lowest step, peering at Cymbril.

"I can't go yet," Cymbril told her, shaken though she was. "I don't have everything I came for."

Miwa made a displeased yowl and bounded two steps higher.

"Go on if you want," Cymbril said. "I have to buy one more thing."

She turned back toward the crowds and tents, wondering how she could find the right place. Well, asking had worked once. She began to search for someone who looked fairly safe—or at least less dangerous than most.

A few women cradling bundles in their arms were lined up at a shop window beneath a sign that read: "CHANGELINGS EXCHANGED—ALL DEALS FINAL." The bundles wriggled and thrashed, and from within the booth came a chorus of wailing and snarling that did not sound good.

Miwa returned, moaning and getting underfoot, determined to herd Cymbril out of the market. When Cymbril clucked her tongue in exasperation and marched toward the nearest booth, Miwa hissed and hurried off in a new direction, lashing her tail.

"Thank you," Cymbril muttered, and followed her.

They passed along the main thoroughfare. It was impossible to see much of anything but the strange Night Marketgoers, shrouded and hooded, winged and furry, some with claws, some with tails twining out from beneath their hems. The aromas of hot food and spices mingled with incense and the odor of wild beasts. Some of the night folk regarded Cymbril surreptitiously or took no notice at all. Some stopped in their tracks to gawk.

So I don't blend in anywhere, she thought. Her shining hair and olive-gold skin set her apart from the Rake folk, and her humanness made her stand out among the Night Marketgoers.

Ahead Miwa turned into a side avenue of fewer shops and less traffic. Leaving the throngs behind, Cymbril followed between two rows of trunks to a round enclosure like a forest clearing.

Four archways allowed entrance through a ring of trees and walls of lattice fence. Roses bloomed all over the trellises—large, heavy-looking roses that mysteriously thrived without the sun. Inside the fence, four tree trunks leaned together, the spaces between them chinked with rocks and mud to form a hut crowned with bare, stubby branches. Moss and leaves spread underfoot, with only limbs above. This was entirely a forest clearing, with no vestige of the Thunder Rake.

Purple light flickered inside the hut. Its single window

was the counter of yet another shop. Miwa growled again, her head low.

Cymbril stooped to pet the cat. "I'll be as careful as I can," she whispered, not liking the look of the place herself. But Loric had assured her that she was in no danger as long as she came to do business. Gathering her courage, she stepped through the fence and crossed the glade, her slippers crinkling the leaves. There was a chill here, the hint of autumn coming behind the summer that was young in the rest of the land.

She stood before the counter, a board with fire-blackened edges laid across the window's stone sill. Inside, she saw a curtained doorway and crowded shelves of jars, bottles, a balance and weights, lidded boxes, and a few urns. The unearthly purple light wavered on the walls. Cymbril couldn't find the light's source. It was a warmthless glow with no lamp to cast it. The shop had a simple herbal smell like that of any kitchen's spice shelf.

She leaned toward the counter, not touching it, trying to see more of the interior on either side. The shopkeeper must be in the back, behind the curtain. Cymbril supposed she should call out but felt suddenly fearful of breaking the silence. The impulse rose in her to leave with the skeleton key and count the evening a success.

Behind her, she saw Miwa hiding outside the trellis, the cat's green eyes just visible through the vines.

Yes, Cymbril thought, *I think I'll go now.*

Turning for a final glance into the shop, she yelped.

Just on the counter's other side, two ancient women sat in chairs—*the* women, the sisters with three eyes between them: Atymnia and Fennella. This was their shop, at the heart of their Night Market. How they'd come to be settled there in a single instant, Cymbril couldn't guess. Needles of ice prickled her spine. They still wore yellow, but not the dingy hue they wore beneath the sun. Their scarves shone with the fire in the eyes of wolves.

The Eye Women spoke one after the other, their words nearly overlapping, as if their minds were intertwined.

"She's come."

"The songstress."

"The chick."

"The Thrush."

"The finder."

"The one who sees."

"With coins in her purse."

"To buy."

"To buy of us, sister."

And both dissolved into laughter, a dry and tiny sound, like spiders coughing: *Ith, ith, ith, ith, ith.*

"F-fair evening," Cymbril stammered. "I've come to buy Nixielixir."

The two withered heads turned toward each other. Then came the laughter again: *Ith, ith, ith.*

"The elixir of Nixies—"

"—under the sea."

"Beauty she seeks."

"Skin like moonlight under the waves."

"Hair that billows in the watery wind, thirty fathoms below."

"Eyes like stars and the wells of the Deep."

"Beauty that hardens the heart like coral."

"But not for herself."

"No, surely, not for herself."

Ith, ith, ith.

Ith, ith, ith, ith, ith.

Cymbril didn't know what to make of the flood of words. As she gazed back and forth between them, she was sure the third eye traveled. The sisters' faces squinted and twisted as they spoke. First one would widen her eyes, exposing two red-veined orbs with ink-black irises. And yet, in the next heartbeat, the same woman had one eye closed and shriveled, and her sister had two eyes. Now right, now left, without using their hands, they passed the shared eye back and forth as they seemed to pass their single mind. Cymbril had the awful notion that it was not the eye that wandered to and fro, but the emptiness of the socket—a hollow well, a black pit of loss that the crones traded and cherished, each desiring to wear it in her head.

With a fearsome suddenness, the sister on the left pounced to her feet and set a small stoppered bottle on the counter. It stood there glinting in the purple light, the dark liquid inside swirling from the motion that had brought it there.

Cymbril stared. There had been no hunting among shelves. She could only conclude that the woman had known beforehand exactly what Cymbril had wanted to buy.

"The price—" said the old woman.

"The moon is half-past full," said her sister.

"So the cost is dearer."

"Six coins."

"Six coins it must be."

Now there was no laughing.

Cymbril nodded, in no mind to question or haggle. She pulled open her coin purse and began to count.

Her heart sank. "I don't have six." She felt around inside the purse, hoping she'd miscounted. But there'd been only seven coins to start with. Two for the skeleton key, with change back, and one to the doorman. She didn't have nearly enough.

Now the other sister had risen and loomed over the counter.

"Not six?" asked one.

"Not six?" demanded the other.

"How many?"

"How much?"

Their wrinkled faces writhed and bunched, staring and squinting.

With a start, Cymbril saw the fat frog beside her, gazing up with reproach.

She took a breath. "I . . . I have four coins. And five stars." She lined up the coins and the stars on the countertop, shaking the purse to be sure she'd missed nothing.

Once more the sisters swiveled their heads to peer at each other. Then the three eyes blazed at Cymbril.

One sister snatched the bottle, and Cymbril was sure she meant to take it away. But instead, she held it out while the other sister scooped up the coins and stars.

"The sale is made," said the first, wiggling the bottle until Cymbril took it.

"The difference is exacted," said the other.

Cymbril knew enough of marketing to question what she'd heard. "What's been exacted?"

"The price," said the second.

"Four moons," said the first.

"Five stars."

"And the difference."

"What difference?" Cymbril asked, looking down at herself. She had the sudden cold fear that she'd be missing a finger or a leg.

"Nothing of yours."

"Nothing you'll miss."

Cymbril wasn't satisfied. She felt angry and more than a little scared. "I have to know, or I'm not buying this. What is exacted?"

Atymnia and Fennella stood like a mass of storm clouds behind the counter.

"The worth of six half-moons," muttered one.

"Six," agreed the other.

"Nothing more," said both sisters together. "All is fair."

"Now go."

"Fair and done."

"Take what is yours."

The sisters sat back down in perfect unison.

Trembling, Cymbril watched them. The fat frog was

uncomfortably close, unblinking, his sides pulsing with his breath. After a long moment, she pulled the drawstring, closing the purse that was still tied to her wrist. From the countertop, she picked up the blue bottle and the twine-bound box that held the key.

Step by step, she backed away from the tree hut, watching the old women in the purple window. When she reached the rose fence and turned away, she was sure she heard, far behind her, a faint *ith, ith, ith.*

The look on Miwa's face said, *I hope you're happy.* For her own part, Cymbril was hoping the doorkeeper wouldn't demand another coin to open the door again on her way out.

Chapter 10

The Exacted Difference

The Rake opened its gate the next morning at Gallander, a settlement that sprawled around the knees of an ancient hill fort. A council hall stood where the fortress had once dominated the summit, and the steep sides of the hill were terraced into gardens. Cymbril's favorite feature of Gallander was the weathered ring of standing stones on an outthrust arm of the hill. The people—possibly giants—who had placed the stones were long vanished, and the circle was draped in a profusion of grapevines. The wine made from these grapes was the chief attraction of Gallander's midsummer festival, or so Cymbril had heard in the market.

When she'd been eight years old, Cymbril had tried to

escape in Gallander. She'd slipped away from her music teacher and crawled off into a field of tall grass. Even now she could remember giggling as she rolled down a slope through the green stems, butterflies and grasshoppers dodging out of her way, while people in the marketplace shouted for her. She'd gotten no farther than the stone circle. It had seemed to call to her with a silent melody, a song she felt deep in her core rather than heard. Itchy from the grass, tired from her escape, she'd drawn up her knees and sat with her back against a rough, cool stone. She'd watched clouds drift in the dazzling blue, changing their shapes. She'd gazed at the lines of soldiers and merchants looking for her, fanned out across the fields. Finally it was one of the Knights Fountainers who had discovered her, speaking kindly as he offered her his hands, and then hoisted her into the saddle of his magnificent black horse with a white star on its forehead. Riding back with him to the market, Cymbril felt she could see the whole world from that saddle, as if it were somehow higher than the soaring decks of the Rake.

On this visit to Gallander, the sky drizzled rain all day, raising white mist from the gardens, filling the air with the smells of slick black leaves and sticks shiny with damp. At the dawn gathering in the ramp bailey, Rombol announced that the market would be held indoors. So as lightning flashed beyond the windows and rain splattered the sills, the merchants scrambled to convert their wagon procession into rows of stalls.

Amid the traffic and shouts, Cymbril skillfully disappeared before she could be given a task. She'd resolved to deliver the Nixielixir early so that she could quit worrying about it. With irony, she thought about what a relief it was to be among mundane merchants again, where no one had wings or tongues that forked.

Even after getting back to her bunk, she'd slept poorly, her mind too full of memories and questions. It still bothered her that the Eye Women had finished the sale without her agreement—and that they'd spoken of the "exacted difference" between the cost of her purchase and the money she had. They'd taken the value of six coins (so they said)—nothing of Cymbril's, nothing she'd miss.

She had examined the blue bottle again and again, holding it up to the light of her stone and pin, pulling out the stopper to sniff its contents. Was it truly safe to give Gerta and Berta an elixir she'd bought from the likes of the sisters? What if it turned them into snails? Worse, what if it was poison?

A fine time to be doubting the plan now, she scolded herself. Loric knew what he was talking about—she would have to trust him on this. When morning had finally come, she'd stuffed her Night Market purchases into her pockets, along with her own two treasures.

Dodging among people with armloads of goods, she hopped up onto a barrel and spied, near one end of the gallery, the cloth dyers' booth. *Perfect.* Berta and her mother were busily arranging the bolts and racks of cloth while Gerta drove their now-empty wagon away toward the ramp that led up to the Hall of Wagons. As Gerta waited in the queue, holding the reins of her swaybacked horse, Cymbril would have all the time she needed. Before moving forward, Cymbril studied the twins' mother, her face careworn and sad beneath her wayward gray hair. What must it be like for her, watching her daughters lose their minds? Unquestionably, the girls were growing more empty-headed all the time. Berta stood with a basket, daydreaming, until her mother scolded her. Gerta dropped the reins and sat counting her fingers. Fortunately, the old horse knew which direction to pull the wagon and where to line up.

One hand gripping the Nixielixir, Cymbril came very close to giving up her plan. Watching the girls and their mother at a distance, something suddenly became clear to her. All this time she'd tried to imagine what the girls *wanted,* supposing that would make them happier. What they *needed* was healing for their minds. Cymbril supposed being beautiful wouldn't hurt the sisters, and maybe happiness would help to restore them. But she couldn't shake off the feeling that she'd bought the wrong thing for them at the Night Market.

Cymbril kept to the shadows until at least twenty carts had moved into line behind Gerta's, screening it from the view of Berta and their mother. Then she sidled past wheels and horses, waving and smiling up at the occasional drivers who greeted her. Coming alongside Gerta's wagon, she seized the handgrip and swung herself into the seat beside Gerta as if she belonged there.

"Good morning, Gerta," she said cheerily.

The taller girl recoiled as if a wild animal had pounced onto the wagon seat. *At least she remembers me,* Cymbril thought. As a deeper color flooded the girl's face and she began to quiver with outrage, Cymbril clutched Gerta's forearm.

"I'm here to apologize," Cymbril said. "I never meant you or your sister any harm, and I'm sorry for all that's happened."

"You—" Gerta spluttered. "You—!"

"I want to give you a present—a good one this time. Then will we be even?"

Since Cymbril had a grip on her right wrist, Gerta swung with her left. Cymbril barely caught the fist in her free hand.

They struggled in the seat, and the wagon creaked. The horse lifted its head and swished its tail.

"Girls, girls!" warned the driver behind them, a man in a slouch hat. Two extremely old brothers in the wagon ahead turned shakily to look over their shoulders.

"Don't mind us," Cymbril called as casually as possible. "We're just talking." Gerta had hold of Cymbril's face now, one finger jammed into her nostril. Growling, Gerta forced her to the seat's edge, trying to hurl her to the ground.

"*Mmmf!* Mlet ngo!" Cymbril struggled to pry Gerta's hand loose from her jaw.

Gerta muttered a string of threats as they both nearly toppled from the seat.

"Girls!" called the man in the slouch hat. "Do I hafta douse you with a bucket o' water?"

"We're f-f-f-fine!" Cymbril grated through clenched teeth. With a heave, she flung Gerta's hand off her face, and the girl's knuckles crashed against the wooden seat back. Gerta yowled.

"Listen to me!" Cymbril seized the hand again before it punched her. "I'm here about your hair!"

Gerta glared, but she held still. "What about my hair?"

The two old men peered owl-eyed from one girl to the other.

"There's a way to make it grow full and shiny." Cymbril rushed to get the words out. "Your sister's, too. And your skin. I have an elixir that will make you both beautiful as the princesses in old stories."

"Little squawking liar!"

"No! No! It's right here." Cymbril dipped her hand into her pocket and pulled out the bottle.

She scooted away, gasping for breath, as Gerta snatched the Nixielixir and stared at it.

Gerta grabbed Cymbril by the collar. "It's nothing but Moonpine dye. What do you take me for?"

"No, it's Nixielixir—I promise!" Cymbril winced as Gerta tightened her grip. "Smell it! Rub a little on your finger! I only want to set things right between us. I never meant to turn you blue. I'm sorry."

Gerta held on tightly but looked again at the bottle. " 'Nixie liquor'?"

Cymbril nodded emphatically. "It's magical."

"Let's go!" shouted the man in the slouch hat, pointing ahead. The wagon line had advanced. The two old brothers shifted back around on their high seat, and Gerta picked up her reins, the bottle clamped between her knees. The horse heaved a sigh and clopped onto the ramp. Now Gerta had to keep her other hand on the brake to prevent the wagon from rolling backward, and Cymbril let out a relieved breath, straightening her clothes.

"Why should I believe you?" said Gerta with a sniff.

"That's up to you." Cymbril's pride was returning now that she'd handed the bottle over. "I went to a lot of trouble to get it. And just so you know, I use Nixielixir myself." She ran her fingers through her hair, letting it swish across her shoulders.

That was a bald-faced lie, but something told her it was the way to get Gerta and Berta to drink the elixir. "Look," she added, "you can go on hating me until the elixir works. What have you got to lose?"

As the horse labored to pull the wagon up the incline, Gerta rode the brake lever. The iron shoes screeched against the axles.

"If it's a trick," Gerta said, "you'll be very sorry."

"And if it's not, will we be squared away?"

After a long, dark glance, Gerta nodded.

"Give me your hand on it."

Reluctantly, Gerta shook Cymbril's hand.

"Have a good market day," Cymbril said, and jumped down from the wagon.

But as she passed the wagon's bed, the glitter of round eyes startled her. There, hidden among a pile of empty sacks, was the fat frog. Cymbril frowned, gazing from the frog to Gerta.

"Oh, that thing's always following us," Gerta said with an air of disgust, glancing over her shoulder. "We're so sick of chasing it away that now we usually just ignore it."

This new fact puzzled Cymbril, but she had too much else to think about. At least it was nice to know the frog sometimes followed around people other than her.

She caught a tongue-lashing from Wiltwain for going missing—and because the right sleeve of her dress was ripped half off. The Overseer turned livid when she said she'd gone to find Gerta. But when Cymbril told him she thought the trouble with the sisters would be over now, Wiltwain looked at her curiously.

"You didn't *hurt* Gerta, did you?" he asked.

"Of course not."

"And you didn't cast a spell and turn her into something nonhuman?"

By the moon and stars, I hope not, she thought. Wiltwain's conjectures often struck uncomfortably close to the truth. "How would I have done that?"

The corner of his mouth twisted. "With you, Cymbril, all things are possible."

"She's fine."

"Well, then, if you've mended the fence, that dress is a small price to pay. Go and change. Since we're indoors, brown is too drab, anyway. Wear the red-and-gold. And comb that hair."

Again Rombol did not keep Loric on display for much of the day. Before noon the Master withdrew him from the market to rest him for the night's journey. From her balcony, Cymbril watched them go, and she was sure Loric glanced up at her with a smile. She envied him. After the mostly sleepless night, she would have liked nothing better than to find her own bed and crawl under the covers.

Rain sluiced down on the ramp outside, making a mire of the fields and roads. The folk of Gallander came in stamping and dripping in sodden cloaks. Cymbril sang them "Blue Were Her Eyes," which had a beautiful melody and was one of the songs that crowds everywhere requested the most. Cymbril had worked her performance of it into a high art. She knew when to pause, when to increase the sound, when to fade—she knew how to shape and color the notes, drawing the deepest shades of meaning from the words. Usually by the end of it, many listeners' eyes were full of tears.

Green were the lane and the leaves above;
Red were the roses around my love.
Black was her hair, her skin like the dew;
Her heart was a fire that warmed me through.
Bright was the sky and golden the land,
Soft was her breath as she clasped my hand,
And blue as the ocean, blue were her eyes.

Red were the banners and crimson the morn;
To arms we rose at the long, loud horn.
Dark was my heart as I went to sea,
Golden the locket she gave to me.
Black was her hair in a scarlet band,
Silver her tears as she clasped my hand,
And blue as the ocean, blue were her eyes.

Fierce was the battle for land and crown,
Bloody the day when the walls came down.
Black were the ravens that followed the fight;
Deep was the prison still as night.
Hope was the ember her image fanned;
In every dream she clasped my hand,
And blue as the ocean, blue were her eyes.

Long were my years in the darkling grave,
Locked in the dungeon beyond the wave;
Fair was the morning that I went free,
Borne by the ship that came for me.
Gold was the light on the well-loved strand.
I knew that soon she would clasp my hand,
And blue as the ocean, blue were her eyes.

Green were the lane and the leaves above;
Red were the roses around my love.
White was her hair and cold the fire;
Strong were her sons by another sire.
Bright was the sky and golden the land,
Silver her tears as she clasped my hand,
And blue as the ocean, blue were her eyes.

Why were love songs written in such a way? Did love never go unhindered? Was it always unfulfilled and inseparable from pain?

And why, when Cymbril sang of young men, did she see only Loric's face? To think of him romantically would be foolishness on the scale of Gerta's and Berta's. Loric was Fey, of a different world—a world as far removed from hers as Mount Aruna from the Sea of Shalii. Still, he had helped her. He did not seem anything like the perilous Sidhe in stories.

Once more, at the risk of missing her own supper, she found herself waiting for Runa and the tray bound for Loric. Cymbril was running out of things with which to pay Runa off. This time she used a silver ring set with a piece of jade. She'd gotten it last year at a market in Highcircle, when a fine lady had stood alone at the end of the day, weeping as she listened to Cymbril's last song. After Cymbril had finished, the lady had torn the ring from a cord about her neck, flung it to the ground at Cymbril's feet, and glided away into the twilight. "May you be better served than I," the lady had said to Cymbril. Picking it up, she'd felt how warm the ring was from resting against the lady's skin.

"Better served"—doesn't she know I am a servant? Cymbril had wondered. Later she understood that the lady had been speaking of love.

Now was the time to part with the ring. She'd never particularly liked it. And she had to know if the skeleton key would really work.

When Cymbril held out the ring, Runa tipped her sunbrowned face to one side. "Do you fancy the Fey boy?"

"No." Cymbril felt her cheeks heating up. "I'm asking him questions, learning things I need to know."

Runa tucked a strand of her hair behind her ear. "He just wants to steal you away to the land inside the mountains. It's what the Fey do, you know. It's why they come among us."

Cymbril took the tray as Runa examined the ring.

"This stone isn't very pretty," Runa said, and then dropped the ring into her pocket.

"No," Cymbril agreed. And then, feeling it was a custom she should uphold, she added, "May you be better served than I."

When she'd slid back the bar and opened the door, Loric bowed to her with his usual politeness and prayed his Fey prayer over the food. She marveled at his patience. How could he refrain from demanding to know if she'd gotten the key?

"Did it go well with Gerta and Berta?" he asked.

"Yes. Thank you."

"Best not to thank me until we see the results." Grinning, he began to eat. "So you went to a Night Market. I wish I could have gone with you."

Checking the hallway for any approach, Cymbril took her father's glowing stone from her pocket, then stepped into the chamber and pulled the door shut. Anyone who came along would see the wooden beam out of its brackets, but this way she and Loric could talk more freely. Watching his face in the magic light, she realized she'd just enclosed herself with him in a very small space. A nervous thrill shot through her.

"That is a lovely one," Loric said, admiring the stone.

She wondered what he might tell her about the blue-green stone, but at the moment she was in a hurry. Having taken the box from her other pocket, she handed it to him. "Here's a present for you. Although you paid for it, so I suppose it's not really a present."

Carefully, he took the box and untied the red twine. But when he looked inside, he frowned.

Cymbril felt a stab of panic. "Is it the wrong kind? Won't it work?"

"For opening this lock, no, it won't work." He reached into the box with his thumb and forefinger and held up a stubby, greasy chicken bone, its gristly ends gnawed clean.

Cymbril seized the box, looked inside, and shook it upside down. It was otherwise quite empty.

"They tricked me!" she said, feeling both sick at heart and furious.

"I doubt the skeletons did," said Loric. "They are generally quite honest. But someone seems to have made a switch." He sighed, setting the chicken bone down on his empty tray.

Cymbril guessed the truth at once. The only time the box had been out of her hand was on the Eye Women's countertop. "The difference has been exacted." The old women had gotten their full price by taking the key. Squeezing her hands into fists, she told Loric the story.

He listened quietly and then nodded. "So actually, you weren't even cheated. That sounds like the way Night Markets are run. There are rules they follow."

Cymbril's anger at the women—at herself for setting down the box—came out as anger against Loric. "Then why didn't you tell me all the rules? I had the key in my hand. If I'd known . . . if I hadn't . . ."

If I hadn't been so determined to get the Nixielixir. Miwa had done everything a cat could do to keep Cymbril away from the Eye Women's shop.

She glared back into Loric's brown eyes and forced herself to calm down. "I'm sorry," she said at last. "I spent all your money."

"You bought the Nixielixir, which is what you went after," he said. "Which was my idea. If it makes the two girls happy, your trip was not wasted and the money was well spent."

Cymbril glanced down, startled, at the touch of his hand on her arm.

"Thank you for buying the key," he said softly.

She nodded, and he withdrew his hand—looking, for the first time, a little self-conscious.

Cymbril took a breath and exhaled. In that moment, gazing at Loric's iron collar and chain, she came to a realization. She lived inside a cage, as she'd known for a long time. It was a nice cage, with friends and comfort, food, clothing, freedom to roam about, and, most of all, the chance to sing—but it was a cage. She wanted out of it.

She wanted freedom badly enough to do whatever it would take.

"There must be another way to get that collar open," she said. "Promise I can come with you, and I'll help you escape."

His large eyes peered at her, the light making gold sparks dance in their depths. For a long time, he said nothing.

What was he thinking? Was he laughing, wondering what more a slave girl could do, when she'd brought back a chicken bone from the Night Market—when she'd never been able to escape herself? Cymbril bit her lip. "Can't I come? Is it such a hard thing to promise?" *Don't you want me to come?*

"Oh, you can come, and I will be glad for your company. It's just that you make it sound like a 'deal,' like something Master Rombol would say."

Cymbril shrugged. "Sometimes deals make sense," she said. "When people give each other their word, both of them try hard. If they try hard together, that's powerful. The Urrmsh rowing together move the Rake." She wrapped her hands around the chain's mooring, the bolted half-ring that anchored it to the wall. It was perfectly immobile, even when she tugged with all her strength.

"I suppose that is true," said Loric. "Well, we have no more money to spend on skeleton keys, so we will need the real one, the key made for this lock. In the daytime Master Rombol's keys are fastened to his belt. At night they hang on a hook beside his bed."

"Did Miwa tell you that, too?"

"I started to tell you before—it is the same way I saw the lights shining in your pocket. Sometimes pictures come to my mind by themselves, and I see objects that are nearby. The pictures are clearer when I am looking for something specific, such as the key."

He paused, chewing a biscuit. Just as he seemed about to say more, boots clunked along the corridor.

Cymbril's heart raced. The footsteps were coming straight for the door.

Loric gave her arm a reassuring squeeze. "You will be all right," he whispered. "Give some thought to how you might get the Master's key, but don't go after it yet. I will tell you when."

Wiltwain the Overseer yanked open the door. He didn't like it when he saw Cymbril kneeling in the gloom beside Loric, but she thought the Overseer also looked relieved. He'd probably been bracing himself to discover Loric missing. "Haven't you a half-dram of sense?" Wiltwain growled at Cymbril. "The cooks can bring him his supper. Go back to your bunk. If you don't have enough chores, we'll find you more."

Loric returned the tray and thanked Cymbril. He'd eaten everything. She was startled at how much time had elapsed in what had felt like a moment.

"Master Wiltwain," Loric said, "will you take me to the relief closet?"

Wiltwain fingered the jangling keys at his own belt and frowned. Cymbril moved out of his way as he leaned against the door frame. "Can't take you anywhere," he said, "until Master Rombol gets back with the key to your collar. He's at a feast with the Master of Gallander."

"This cannot wait," said Loric.

Wiltwain scratched his ear. "Cymbril, bring us a scullery bucket."

Cymbril bowed and hurried away with the tray. So Loric

was right about the key—if Wiltwain himself didn't have a spare, there was only one that could open the lock.

In the dark watches, Cymbril awoke. The only light was the dim yellow glow of the hall's lamp leaking around the edges of her door. She rubbed her face, wondering what had woken her. Probably the blanket—the air was too close and hot for covers. But as she pushed the ragged bedding aside, she heard a sound: Rombol's hound barking somewhere on a lower deck. She raised her head to listen.

It wasn't Bale's moon bark, nor did it sound like the way he upbraided cats who got on his bad side. There was real anger and urgency in his tone, and at times he broke into a *yi-yi-yiii* that Cymbril had never heard.

But the Rake was rolling as usual, and even Cymbril's curiosity couldn't overcome her drowsiness. Tonight she was happy not to be at the center of things, where the barking was aimed and running footsteps converged. She rolled over and sighed, glad to be comfortable and alone in the dark, without a duty or an expectant crowd to entertain.

After a while, Bale was quiet again, and Cymbril was asleep.

Two nights later, after a bustling market in Grovender, Cymbril was mending the sleeve she'd torn in her scuffle with Gerta. The decks jolted, and the Rake began its journey to Banburnish Crossing. For the past two mornings and evenings, Cymbril had been trying to catch a glimpse of the Curdlebree girls, but every time she tried to slip away to the cloth dyers' stall, someone had found her and put her to work carrying this or toting that.

Still wearing her singing dress—fine green velvet brocaded in gold—she sat on her bunk with her feet tucked beneath her. The Rake's arms squealed and boomed, squealed and boomed, pulling the city wagon into darkness. The decks tilted, and Cymbril guessed the wheelman had turned from the road's verge, setting a course over rain-soft, uneven ground.

It made sense that Rombol would pay eight hundred fifty gold pieces for a Sidhe who could see in the dark. The Rake could not travel on the roads. Its steel claws would demolish any pavement they crossed, churning up cobbles like the soil of a plowed field. Nor could Rombol cut across farms or mow down the King's forests. The Rake must follow the wildest country where no one built or planted, where bogs and chasms threatened even the Rake's giant wheels. Torches on the bow did not drive back much of the night. Rombol groused bitterly on moonless evenings when travel became impossible, costing the merchants good business days.

Cymbril gazed deep into the glowing stone from her father. Sometimes she pretended the stone was a window through time and space, that somewhere on the other side of its blue-green fire, her father was also holding it, looking deep inside it just as she was. She would turn the stone and stare harder, hoping for a glimpse of his face.

Loric would be on the Rake's bow this evening, searching the blackness ahead and warning the helmsman of obstacles. If Cymbril was to free him, the first step would be to learn how he was guarded when he worked.

She'd take extra measures for secrecy tonight. She rummaged in her trunk for the long, hooded cloak she wore when it rained. Its dark gray color would help her blend into the shadows. With the hood pulled low over her face, she closed her door softly and flitted through the least-traveled alleys, heading for the prow.

Chapter 11

The Star Shard

For most of the way, Cymbril followed the edge of the second-highest deck. She preferred to be in the fresh air, and the profusion of apple and pear trees growing in the deck's deep soil beds draped masking branches above her.

It was a clear night under a waning crescent moon, the stars brilliant and the air warm, scented of mud and the mustiness of a swamp. The Rake's claws, slicing into the marshes, made softer noises than usual. Water gurgled around the wheels. Beyond the rail, Cymbril glimpsed the clumped heads of trees brushing the lower decks. The rolling plain of moon-washed leaves stretched around the giant vessel for as far as she could see, parting before the bow, whispering along the sides. With its wheels and claws hidden among the trunks below, the Rake seemed a real ship plowing the waves of a silvery sea. Crickets sang in the Rake's groves, while tens of thousands shrilled back from the forest outside.

Cymbril padded up a stairway, avoiding the steps that squeaked. On the second step from the top, she recognized the shape of the fat frog. As she edged past him, he watched her with his wide mouth turned down, as if she had no right to be using his stairway.

The bow was darker than usual, for which she was grateful. Sidling between the vine-covered wall of a grape arbor and the winery, she spied a row of barrels and crouched behind them. Raising her head, she saw a single lantern flickering on a pole and four cloaked figures at the very front of the foredeck.

One was unmistakably Rombol, thick and hulking. Wan light glinted on the armor and helmets of two men-at-arms. Past them, on the triangular pulpit sticking out from the prow, glimmered a small shape that could only be Loric. His pale hand rested on the rail, and the chain around his neck jingled as he took a few steps to the right. The row of torches stood unlit in their brackets along the front rail.

"The land falls away there," said Loric, pointing. "We should steer to the left."

Rombol turned, and Cymbril hunched lower. But the

Master was looking above her, toward the wheelhouse. "Five clacks to the shield arm," he called to the pilot. The Rake began a creaking turn.

Rombol set his hands on Loric's shoulders. "That's it, boy! Carry on just like this until you see the guard towers of Banburnish. We should arrive before sunup. Get us there safely, and you'll have fresh blueberries and the whole day to sleep."

"I understand the task, Master," Loric said pleasantly.

Chuckling, Rombol patted the Sidhe's head, then gazed sternly at the two guards. He unhooked a large key from the ring at his belt and handed it to one of the men. "If there's any trouble, don't stop to think. Wake me."

With a final glance out over the landscape, he strode in Cymbril's direction.

Ducking, she scooted back farther into the dark space at the building's corner. As she tried to wriggle farther out of sight, the dry grape leaves crackled beneath her feet.

She froze in place. Ten paces away, on the other side of the barrels, Rombol stopped walking. She could hear his cloak rustle as he turned, hunting for what had made the sound. His breath hissed in and out through his red nose, and Cymbril wondered if he could hear her pounding heart.

Something scrabbled in the leaves to her left. From the corner of her eye, she caught a flash of movement.

Miwa darted from the gloom, hopping stiff-legged, her silvery tail bristling. She arched her back and batted the air as if playing with an invisible mouse. Having bounded to the top of a windlass post, she sat licking a paw and turned indifferent eyes on Rombol.

The Rake's Master grumbled at the cat and stumped away to his quarters. Speaking quietly, the guards settled onto a bench a dozen paces behind Loric. Miwa groomed herself, glanced once toward Cymbril with what looked like a smile, and began an agile stroll along the rail.

Cymbril let out her breath and waited for her heart to slow down. She'd managed to get Miwa a dish of cream from the kitchens on the evening after their Night Market adventures, but she still felt indebted to the cat—and now Miwa had helped her again.

Cymbril edged forward once more, being very careful where she placed her hands, knees, and feet. So the key stayed with whoever was guarding Loric. The elf boy's chain looped to the railing beside him where the second manacle was fastened around a sturdy upright post.

"I see low hills and the river channel on the left," Loric reported to the guards. "The trees are scattered now. Once we pass this thicket, we should swing right."

A guard relayed the information to the wheelhouse.

Cymbril sat back, listening to the chop of the claws, watching the scrub trees march toward the bow to be flattened. Often the Rake followed paths it had gouged on previous trips, ugly swaths through the wilderness. But Rombol was always trying new shortcuts, striving to make better time.

Studying the pulpit and the guards, Cymbril had an idea. Even in mud, the Rake's arms made considerable noise, as did the crunching trees and shrubs. Tongue between her teeth, she took one more look around and slipped back the way she'd come.

The first stairway took her down beside a tower filled with wheat to a half-level beneath the top deck, a hive of low-ceilinged hallways and bins for storing tools and grain. No light filtered from beneath the counting master's door. Slinking past it, Cymbril heard faint snores from within.

"*Moowwrrr,*" said a voice behind her—the suspicious challenge of a cat, loud in the cramped space. But when Cymbril rubbed her fingers together, the large yellow tom nuzzled her and purred. It glided along with her as she tiptoed up a flight of three steps into a small chamber. She searched for the passage she wanted. There—a short, narrow duct leading straight to the prow. The far end was closed with a hatch, hinged at the top. Through a glass pane, Cymbril looked out at the dim marshland sliding toward her: stunted trees, stands of bush and hedge, and faint moonlight glittering on pools, on ribbons of stream.

Two deadbolts fastened the hatch at its bottom edge. Working by feel, she pushed the shanks back through their tracks. Carefully, she found the cold handle and pulled the hatch toward her. A rusted hook on the frame slipped into a ring on the ceiling. The tomcat regarded Cymbril doubtfully as she crawled out onto a tiny square platform with no rails— a shelf on the clifflike prow of the Rake, nearly five stories above the ground—six, counting the empty space beneath the wagon city's axles. To the left and right, the enormous claws swung on their tree-trunk arms, first one, then the other, slamming into the turf. Straight above Cymbril, but well beyond her reach, was the underside of the pulpit on which Loric stood.

A heavy iron pulley hung there. Cymbril had watched the Rake's merchants hoist flour sacks up from the ground. She had never wanted to be the man who crouched on this platform with a long-handled hook, snagging the sacks and hauling them aboard.

But here she was, and the platform was much, much higher than it looked from below. She clutched her collar shut and held on to the hatch frame. Maybe this hadn't been such a good idea. It was like flying—empty air all around, and the world unfolding, a thousand shades of gray and blue, moisture-laden wind, and her hair and cloak whipping.

From a safe distance in the passage behind her, the cat's eyes advised her to come in. The moon was lowering toward the west. Treetops swayed in the breeze. Away over the silver-etched boughs, an owl circled. As the Rake lurched through a rut, Cymbril almost shrieked.

Don't look down, she told herself. She closed her eyes and concentrated on finding just the right volume for her voice.

"Loric?"

She counted slowly to five, holding her breath. Then she tried again, a fraction louder. "Loric? Can you hear me?"

The cat glanced over his shoulder into the dark hallway and tilted his ears: forward, then back, then one forward and one back.

"Cymbril."

Had it been Loric's voice or the breeze? She rose to her knees, straining to hear. The wheels splashed into shallow water, throwing up gouts of mud against the underboards: *whump, whump, whump.*

"Stone. Stoo-oone."

Yes! It *was* Loric's voice, very soft. It was trickier for him to speak, Cymbril knew, with nothing but air between him and the guards. But what was he saying? *Stone?*

"Fooore . . . heeaad . . ."

Stone? Forehead? Cymbril wanted to hear words—but these seemed random, nonsensical. Was she only imagining them?

"A little to the left!" said Loric, much more loudly. Then he whispered again, "Forehead."

She nearly forgot to hang on as the bow yawed to the left. She blinked up at the pulpit's underside, then looked around herself. There were trees, more empty air than she cared for, and down in the dark, a great deal of mud. But "stone" was the one material she couldn't see anywhere.

Cymbril drew a breath, and her hand darted to her pocket. "Stone" could only mean one thing.

Holding her father's stone tightly, she gazed into its depths, which shone with a deep aquamarine, brighter than she'd ever seen it. *Forehead.* Without thinking, she raised the stone to her brow.

It was smooth on her skin, warm from her pocket, and hard—exactly as it felt in her hand. But in a heartbeat, it was as if a door had swung open in her mind—as if she were at one end of a tunnel in the air.

Cymbril!

Loric's voice: not through her ears, but inside her head, as clear as if he were beside her.

Now you can hear me, and I can hear y—

Startled, Cymbril pulled the stone away. Silence. When she pushed the stone back to her brow again, Loric's voice returned.

Are you there? Don't speak aloud.

Yes, she answered, pressing her lips together, careful not to use her voice. She only thought the words. *Yes, I can hear you. Is this Sidhe magic?*

It is. We can speak with our thoughts through this stone you carry, if we are close together.

Cymbril wanted to laugh with delight. *And no one else can hear us?*

No one. Aloud, Loric told the guards the Rake should veer left again to avoid what might be quicksand.

Cymbril grinned at the cat, who had curled into a circle, eyes nearly closed, paws warming his nose.

What is this stone? Cymbril asked in her mind. *Where could my father have gotten it?*

Did your father give it to you?

He left it for me.

And I suppose no one has ever been able to take it away from you, though several have tried.

Cymbril nodded, still smiling with joy at this freedom to speak under the guards' very noses. Then, remembering Loric couldn't see her nod, she thought, *That's right.*

It was true. Once a boy, one of the kitchen slaves, had tripped her with a broomstick and grabbed the stone from her hand. The boy dashed away to hide, and she had run screaming to Master Rombol, who'd told her grumpily to go to her bunk, that it would be all right. Weeping all the way back, Cymbril had been sure the stone was gone forever—but when she'd opened her door, it was waiting for her, glowing on the middle of her bed. Another time a dour old teabunk seamstress had snatched her hairpin and said it was too valuable for a little girl to wear around, that she would "keep it safe" for Cymbril. Again Cymbril had howled—but even before she reached her room, she'd found the pin back in her hair. That's when she realized the treasures were more magical than she'd guessed, for they could not be stolen. Rombol, she was sure, had tried to take them away first of all—and probably so had the woman with the red scarf and hairy chin.

Cymbril could, however, put the treasures somewhere and walk away, and they would not come back to her. She'd cautiously tried that with both. As to whether she could accidentally lose them, she had no way of knowing—unless it happened, and the thought of that made her very unhappy.

The stone, Loric said, *is a Star Shard. It's full of starlight. Star Shards are very rare. They fall from the sky. I suspect your father found it. The hairpin was made with Fey magic.*

But, Cymbril began, *how could my parents—?*

Cymbril, only a Sidhe can find a Star Shard.

She thought about that. Surely her father couldn't have bought a treasure so precious—who would ever sell it?

And "Cymbril" is a Sidhe name.

Cymbril felt a rush of emotion, as if a soundless chord of music had passed through her. She looked at the long, lithe fingers of her hand on the hatch frame. Glimpsing her flying hair, she understood at last why it was of a different hue than anyone else's. Tears spilled down her cheeks. It was as if she'd found something that had been lost for years and years, but all the while it had been close by. Mouth and nose to the wind, she inhaled the earthy scents. Now she knew why she felt at times so apart from the other slaves. She knew why she had trouble understanding the deepest hearts of even the humans she liked. If she was Fey, it also explained why she could find hidden magical corridors. But she couldn't see in the dark.

You have many human qualities, too, Loric said. *Your mother must have been of the Second Folk. But your father was one of my people. That makes you a Halcyon Fey, with the blood of both.*

The half-hidden waters glittered. Everything in the dark land looked different—the air smelled different, felt different on her skin—and everything called to her. Suddenly, the enormous Rake was not nearly big enough to contain her. *Tell me that it's really true,* she said through the stone.

Look into a mirror, Loric said. *You have blue eyes. If in one of them you see a streak of brownish gold, that's a sure sign of a Halcyon.*

If she'd been on a safer perch, Cymbril would have danced. She knew she had such a streak. Her parents' faces became a little clearer in her mind. Escape from this place felt all the more important, and she was certain there must be a way. It was as if discovering more about her past assured her that she would have a future. She came closer to understanding Loric's calm—his patience, his fearlessness of locks and chains.

Nor had she missed hearing the fact that Loric knew the color of her eyes.

She felt something in her mind—a warmth, a comforting sense of someone nearby but not intrusive—and at once she jerked the stone away from her head, mortified that another person could be sharing every thought she had.

She held it against her chest, half afraid to use it again. She was too full of thoughts and feelings—they all threatened to come spilling out as laughter in the piercing dark, on this precarious perch above the world, with the treetops spread out like green-black clouds and the low moon soaring.

She glanced back at the cat. His head was raised, the tip of his tail twitching.

Cymbril wanted to see Gorhyv Glyn, Loric's home. One way or another, she would get the key to his collar. She put the stone to her brow to tell him so.

Cymbril! he cried out in her mind. *Get out of there quickly!*

What is it?

There's danger. Master Rombol's hound, and something . . . just GO!

Her pulse quickened. She shoved the stone into her pocket. The cat was on his feet now, facing the black interior and making a soft, unhappy sound. Cymbril scrambled in through the hatch and unhooked the door. It thumped shut. She clawed the bolts into place. The cat preceded her up the passage, ears flat, body crouching.

Where the hall led into the chamber of the three steps, the tom sat bristling and tense, his head pushed forward just enough to peep around the corner. Cymbril waited behind him, still hidden.

A terrible barking shuddered the walls. Toenails clacked

on planks, and something heavy crashed and rolled across the floor.

Cymbril didn't dare to move. She heard a grunting snort—something like the voice of a pig, only deeper, *bigger*. Footfalls crossed the chamber, sending vibrations through the planks under her knees. Cabinet doors rattled. Barrels tipped.

The grunting noise moved farther away, and Bale pursued it, barking savagely.

A tin fell clattering from a shelf, and silence returned.

Staring at the cat, Cymbril gathered her cloak around her, catching her breath. As doors opened in the distance and merchants began to run and shout, the cat dashed off into the shadows.

Cymbril sprinted back to her room. As she passed, she saw that the chamber of the three steps was demolished, barrels and crates broken everywhere.

Shutting the door of her bunk, she glanced around the room in the glow of the Star Shard and tried to stop trembling. She changed quickly into her nightclothes and stowed what she'd been wearing in her trunk. As she dived under the covers, footsteps approached her door.

Someone opened it without knocking. Firelight shone on the walls. Cymbril wondered if she should pretend to be asleep. No—she was a light sleeper. She raised her head and blinked groggily into the light. It was Rombol.

"You're here," he said, glancing around the small berth.

"Yes," she said with an air of confusion.

"And you know nothing of this hurly-burly?"

She rubbed an eye. "What hurly-burly?"

Rombol touched the candlestick on her bedside stand. The wick, of course, was cold. "Never mind," he said. "Sleep. Banburnish Crossing at dawn. Your red dress." Shooting a last dubious look at her, he went out and closed the door.

Cymbril sank back into the bedding. *They always assume I'm behind everything,* she thought. *Well, who can blame them?*

Experimentally, she put the Star Shard against her brow and called out to Loric in her mind. No answer came, even after several tries. Loric had said that the communication worked only if they were near each other. The distance now must be too great, but she'd wanted to be sure.

Cymbril lay still in the darkness. What had Bale been chasing? What had passed through the chamber beneath the prow? It was a long time before she drifted off.

Chapter 12

Metamorphoses

In Banburnish Crossing, Loric wasn't paraded out for the crowds to admire but was allowed to sleep in the Rake as Rombol had promised. Cymbril didn't need to stand in a wagon bed to sing. Banburnish had a platform stage at one end of the marketplace outside the town gate. She also had more chances to rest than usual, since a troupe of jugglers and acrobats shared the stage with her. Rombol was glad of their presence—they helped to swell the throngs of townsfolk and farmers. The performers in their parti-colored costumes tumbled, flipped each other in aerial somersaults, and rode on each other's shoulders in imitation of jousting knights.

It was a delight to be in the sunlight and air. Shreds of

white cloud rode what must be a mighty wind in the upper sky, though the breezes wandered gently through fields and orchards. In such intensity of sunshine, Cymbril was less sure of what she'd heard in the night. Everything seemed ordinary this morning, everyone behaving normally. Bale ambled across the market, exploring its thousand scents.

There were pigs in a pen on the Eaves deck, one story down from the Rake's top. Probably a pig had gotten loose last night and gone tearing through the forward chambers. Cymbril knew from experience that the most common things could be frightening in the dark, especially if they turned up in unexpected places. At any rate, whatever had happened, it looked as if Rombol and his crew had gotten to the bottom of it.

She watched the cloud shadows gliding over roads, gardens, and fencerows. No barriers stopped the shadows of clouds. They needed no keys, could change into any shapes they wished, never had to explain themselves, and no one told them what colors to wear.

Lost in her musings, she studied the Rake. It towered like a gray-green mountain. Where Rombol's market city came and stood, the landscape changed for a day. Trees bunched thick along its upper decks. Its timbers had baked and frozen year on year, soaked by rains and brushed by the passing woods of the world. Nets of ivy and green fungus blanketed its walls, where birds roosted and pecked after insects.

Cymbril smiled, more aware of the Rake's abundant life than she'd ever been. Twenty-three hundred souls made their home aboard it (counting merchant families and slaves, but not counting the Armfolk, animals, or anyone she'd seen at the Night Market). The Rake's dwelling quarters were full. New merchants could take up residence only when others retired, all subject to the approval of Master Rombol, who leased them space and collected a share of their profits.

It seemed so pointless, their life of selling and tallying. What good was a mountain of gold? Having one only made a person want a second mountain or a third. The sun and the trees belonged as much to a peasant as to a king—if only one had the freedom to walk beneath them. Shut within their stalls, the merchants did not allow that freedom to their slaves or even to themselves.

During a rest break, Cymbril sat on a rock, breathing the scent of tilled soil and letting the breeze flutter her hair. A falcon turned in lazy circles high up in the blue. Beside Cymbril's hand, a fat green caterpillar crawled across the stone. She knelt to watch it.

The worm moved steadily, crossing the small world of the boulder's surface just as the Rake navigated the larger land. *Are you going to turn into a butterfly?* Cymbril asked the worm in her mind. *Do you want to change, or do you like the way you are?*

She sighed, telling herself she was being foolish. The worm could not choose to stay a worm.

Her eyelids were drooping when a shadow blocked the sun. In the middle of a yawn, she looked up into the face of Master Rombol.

"You look tired today," he said, eyeing her from beneath the brim of his plush, tasseled hat. "Didn't you sleep well last night?"

"Well enough, Master." She tried to sound as cheerful as Loric always did. "This sunshine makes me sleepy."

He seemed about to say more, but a fine lady called to him from across the greensward, and he waved and strode in that direction, suddenly congenial.

Cymbril was given lunch in the Kettle Tent, where the cooks sold their famous fourteen varieties of soups and stews to the crowds. Having eaten her fill, she grew drowsier than ever and was in no hurry to get back to her stage. As she circled the market's edge, basking in the warmth and brightness, an odd sight stopped her in her tracks.

On a grassy hill, a procession threaded among peach trees. Cymbril shielded her eyes against the glare. At first she thought people were playing a game, though they seemed too old for follow the leader. These were youths—all boys, except for the leaders, who were two maidens with shining golden hair that cascaded to their waists.

Cymbril cocked her head. Some of the boys were Rombol's people, merchants' sons. Some appeared to be local folk. But the lovely, laughing girls . . . they wore aprons and plain dresses, not the gowns Cymbril would have expected from the look of their elegant faces and alabaster skin. Whichever way the girls turned, the line of boys followed, shoving each other, their hats in their hands, all vying for the maidens' attention.

Peering again at the nearer girl's face, Cymbril felt her breath stop. If she'd been carrying an armload of the finest porcelain vases, she would have dropped it.

She was looking at the Curdlebree sisters.

Cymbril stared, her eyes and mouth open wide. She fingered a lock of her hair and compared it to the magnificent hair of the two girls. The Nixielixir had definitely worked. She supposed she should be happy—and relieved that she hadn't poisoned the sisters or turned them into newts—but she was too stunned to feel much of anything. "You're welcome," she muttered at last. "I'd say we're plenty even now."

Banburnish was another two-day market, and the Armfolk trudged to the river ravine for the night. On the way, Urrt sat and listened to a few of Cymbril's songs. "You haven't come to the Pushpull Chamber lately, little thrush," he said, when the press of villagers had left her and were applauding a fire juggler.

Cymbril locked her hands around his wrist and dangled. He lifted her high above the ground, as he had since she was a little girl. Her weight was still nothing to Urrt, no matter how tall she grew. "I know, and I've missed you all." She lowered her voice. "But I'm going to help the Fey boy escape. Urrt, I've found out something. My father was one of the Sidhe."

"That he was," said Urrt, his wide brow wrinkling. "A Dweller Under Stars. I thought you knew that, nightingale. Ah, I always forget that you do not understand our songs. But escape—that's a dangerous thing to do. Master Rombol has dogs and soldiers." He crooked his elbow, and Cymbril sat in the bend, her feet swinging.

"It's not safe," she agreed. "But we have to try. Loric doesn't belong here any more than I do."

Urrt gazed across the crowded market, his huge eyes slowly blinking. "That's true," he rumbled at last. "Very true. So you mean to go with him. Yes, that's as it should be."

A sudden pang of regret shot through her. She had mentioned the escape casually, but surely Urrt would miss her. She would miss him. "Are you sad?" she asked.

He seemed to ponder the question. "No, not when I think of you among Loric's people. We Urrmsh sing our songs, and we push and pull, all together. You belong with your own flock, little bird." He lowered her to the ground and bent close. "On the night when we're nearest the Fey country, if you get him loose from that chain, flee down to the aft hold. A hatch there will be open."

Cymbril smiled and hugged his broad hand.

At the long day's end, Cymbril hurried to Loric's room on her way to her own, counting on the tumult of everyone's return to give her a few moments. No one was in the hallway outside his bolted door. To use the Star Shard, Loric had said, she and he must be near each other. Pressing it to her forehead, she silently called, *Loric, are you there?*

I'm here. His mind-voice sounded sleepy.

Quickly, Cymbril told him of the hatch Urrt would open.

That's good, he said, *but getting the key won't be easy. I'm working on a plan. Gorhyv Glyn is still several days away. You'd better not come to the bow tomorrow night. Something was there last night. Did you see it?*

No, but I heard it. So Loric didn't think the grunting thing had been a runaway pig. *What do you suppose it was?*

It didn't feel like any animal I know. If I get a chance to talk to a cat, I'll see if it can tell us more. Until we find out what it was—and whether it's still on the Rake—I don't think you should leave your room at night.

Cymbril didn't like that idea at all. She'd already been working on a strategy for sneaking back to the bow. Embarrassed that her thoughts might make her seem stubborn and childish, she hurried to her next question. *I haven't been able to guess. How did you overcome the touch of iron?*

With patience, he said. *Not being able to touch worked metals seemed a disadvantage, so I decided to see what might be done. In our land, there is a marshy meadow that was the place of a great battle long ago, when the doors of the Fey world were open. All sorts of old mysterious treasures lie half-buried, tangled in the grasses' roots: broken swords, shields, horses' shoes, and wagon wheels.*

I found some iron nails there, put one in my pocket, and carried it for a cycle of the moon, then added another. I brought my hand closer and closer to an old, rusting helmet until I could touch it. Then I touched it for longer and longer each day until there was no more pain. I would feel better without this collar on, but I can endure it.

She thought about the explanation. Loric's patience was like the lever the Urrmsh had described, the one long enough to turn over a mountain.

Finally, she told Loric that the Nixielixir had worked.

I noticed. Well done. Are the sisters happy now?

I'm sure they are. She pulled the stone quickly away from her brow. *Of course you noticed,* she thought privately. *You're a boy.*

Chapter 13

The Threshold of the Wild

The second day in Banburnish Crossing crept by. In the afternoon Master Rombol brought Loric out again. As the people petted him, Loric's smile began looking a little strained. Patience has limits, Cymbril told herself. Collars have to come off.

By evening talk of the Curdlebree sisters had spread to every corner of the Rake. None of the young men were of any use to their parents. They left booths unattended, ignored customers, spilled grain, and made mistakes when counting money. Cymbril got no supper that evening and spent a very unpleasant time in the garrison room, explaining again and again to Rombol and Wiltwain where she'd gotten the magic potion that had transformed the sisters. She made no mention of Loric, but implied rather that she'd found the enchanted forest deck just as she'd found the hallway off Tinley. And she was distinctly vague on the subject of coins.

The more she talked of the Night Market, the angrier Rombol became, insisting that no such things took place aboard his Rake. When Cymbril led the Master and the Overseer to the court of the spidery statue, of course the second door was gone without a trace. There was only the ominous door to the dwelling of the Eye Women, with the hatch for the frog.

"Ask the women who live there," Cymbril said in desperation. "They're in charge of the Night Market."

"You will speak of it no more," Rombol ordered, leading her away with a tight grip on her arm. He was so angry this time that he consigned her to the kitchens, where she spent two days peeling potatoes, scrubbing pots, stirring, carrying flour bags, sifting, emptying slop—and whatever else the cooks could find for her to do. She missed the markets at Andridge and Crallagh, while Master Rombol made his point that the Rake could do perfectly well without its Thrush. Cymbril had to sleep in a chamber shared by seven other kitchen maids, all on pallets and under the beady gaze of Mistress Reech, a sharp-chinned cook who dozed in a chair and awoke if one of the girls so much as rolled over.

On the second evening, just as the Rake rolled out of Crallagh, there came a loud blaring of trumpets, and the wagon city drew to a halt. Servants ran through the kitchen, shouting of knights and banners and a company of riders in fine coats and furs.

Cymbril dashed with the other girls to the outer railing. They were just in time to see the splendid entourage coming aboard, men in velvet hats and tasseled cloaks, riding horses with braided manes. "The King's household!" someone exclaimed. "They're here on business for the King himself!"

Not supposing her punishment could get any worse, Cymbril sidled away as the other girls began to speculate. She had not far to go to reach the ramp bailey. Hiding would have been pointless. A crowd of merchants and servants bunched at the balcony rails, jostling for a view of the grand floor below. Cymbril found a place from which she could peer down at a portly, bearded man with a brilliant red feather in his hat. As Rombol and his closest associates listened, the man read from a long scroll.

Most of what he read were flowery, formal greetings and establishments of His Majesty's greatness and generosity. But slowly Cymbril pieced together what was happening.

The King's scout had chanced to see the Curdlebree sisters in Banburnish Crossing and had ridden straightaway to the capital to inform the King, who was seeking brides for his two middle sons. Indescribable beauty, it seemed, was the only requisite for princes' wives. The King's envoys had come to shower Master Rombol with gifts and to ask for the hands of Berta and Gerta in marriage to the Princes Rowan and Jeldspar.

Rombol gave an impassioned speech about how the beautiful Curdlebree sisters had long been the pride of the Thunder Rake—and how they were as gentle, sweet, and clever as they were comely. Through a tangle of their admirers, Cymbril glimpsed Gerta and Berta, who blushed and beamed and fiddled with their hair. Their mother, laughing giddily and fanning herself, swooned twice.

When asked if they would consent to His Majesty's invitation to come at once to the palace, the Curdlebrees all three nodded vigorously, and the mother swooned again.

That very night Cymbril was let out of prison. Wiltwain came by the kitchen with orders for her to return to her old bunk. He gave no explanations but only gazed once at her and said, in his business-like tone, "Sea-blue dress tomorrow, with the belt of coral."

Back in her own bed again, Cymbril rubbed her face with callused hands and laughed and cried herself to sleep. *I've set three people free of this place,* she was thinking. *Four, count-ing Hysthia Giltfeather. And none of them was Loric or me.*

Next came the town of Fencet, a short half-night's journey away over mostly level meadows. The Rake's market there was poorly attended, and the merchants didn't bother unloading their finer wares. Fencet's people had little money to spend. They struggled to scratch out meager crops from hillsides above the gloomy Groag Swamp. Cymbril was happier to sing for these plain folk, for the songs seemed to encourage them.

Truth be told, she was happy to be singing again in the sun and fresh air, and not working in a sweltering kitchen.

Near the day's end, an old man hobbled toward her on a crutch. He'd sat under a tree all afternoon, listening to her sing as he worked on something in the grass. Now Cymbril saw it was a long necklace woven of swamp flowers, pale pur-ple and glistening white in the dusk. With a toothless grin, the man draped the garland around her neck and tottered away. Cymbril's throat felt tight as she called her thanks. This was a much different sort of gift than when the fine lady in High-circle had flung her ring into the dirt and told Cymbril to keep it. The old man had made this garland for her.

It was hard to sleep that night as swamp birds cawed, as the Rake forged across sandbanks and mires. Cymbril longed to prowl the decks for a peek outward between the tree branches on Eaves Lane or from a hatchway along Clerestory. But even she was tired of anything that might lead to trouble.

Counting things could make a person drowsy, so after a few hundred griffins, she thought of the names of all the Armfolk she knew, then the names of all the cats. Lulled by the scent of the flower necklace above her bed, she was just listing the cats on the Rake's second level, front half, when she floated off to sleep.

Rombol fairly bounced with satisfaction the next day. The Thunder Rake had arrived in Ardle, a hamlet the wagon city normally didn't reach until its returning loop after many days farther east.

Rising onto her toes in a wagon bed, Cymbril let the early breeze tickle her face. Ardle stood on a ridge, where the country dropped away on all sides. To the south lay the higher trough of the Groag Swamp, through which the Rake had come. To the east, the ridge slanted away to other villages under a haze of morning mist. But on the north and west, the slopes sagged into a gray tangle of knotted trees and sluggish waterways, shadowy even in the morning. A brooding lowland swamp stretched like the ugliest of carpets for three leagues and more before the ground rose again into cleaner hills.

This was the Lower Groag—"Weepwallow," they called it in the surrounding towns, a part of the true Witching Wild. Only a few roads led through its more passable regions, and Cymbril had often heard Rombol complain about the detours it imposed. The old cooks and servers said deep in the Wild lived robber kings who dwelt in stone castles grander than that of the King himself. And there were beasts in the swamps that made bears seem as puny as the Rake's cats. That might or might not be true, but to be sure, this was Wildhair's country. Poisonous bogs were her lawns. The howling of wolves lulled her to sleep, if she slept at all. As always, Cymbril felt a tremble in her chest at the very thought of Wildhair, and the vision of the Lady's cloaked riders filled her mind.

Brigit. In her preoccupation with everything else, she'd almost forgotten that Brigit had been at the Night Market, too—and had called Cymbril by name. "You've grown," Brigit had said. So they must have met when Cymbril was younger. Cymbril had no memory of the meeting, and it was maddening, like a voice she could not quite hear. But hadn't Wildhair's messenger looked familiar on that first night, when the Rake had stopped for her? Cymbril wished there were some magic that could show her the past.

She had sprinkled her flower necklace with water, and it was still fresh—a perfect match for the lavender dress she wore. The blossoms wreathed her in a cloud of fragrance.

The men of Ardle busied themselves in building a wooden lookout tower, so the marketgoers were not as plentiful as the merchants had hoped. It gave Cymbril a chance to crawl behind a wagon and eat the rolls, plums, and meat pie she'd been given for lunch.

There was no longer a need to listen for the stealthy approach of the Curdlebree twins—no reason to fear a chunk of firewood landing in her lap. Would the sisters be happy as princesses? Would the King's sons be happy with *them?* What, she wondered, would they possibly have to talk about? But maybe princesses weren't expected to talk. If all they had to do was squeal in delight when presented with hair ribbons, then maybe it was a good arrangement for everyone.

She was sipping a crock of cool milk and thinking she'd ask for biscuits and cream tomorrow when she heard voices on the other side of the wagon.

Master Rombol and Wiltwain were discussing business. Cymbril drew up her knees and listened.

"*Seeing* isn't the problem," Wiltwain said. The wagon lurched as he propped a foot on it. "We could plow through Weepwallow by daylight without the elf boy, and it would still be a deathtrap. And don't we have enough to worry about, with—?"

"There are ways," said Rombol. Paper crinkled. "Drier ways, marked on the map. See? I have the safe paths traced in red ink. The Groag is a shortcut to everywhere!"

"Of course it is. That's why the Lady makes her home there, with the snakes and the water rats. And she's not alone. Every cutthroat who eludes the King's knights hides down there. The ones tough enough to survive become Wildhair's soldiers. Some say the dead ones join her army, too."

"We've nothing to fear from the Huntress," said Rombol. "If we learn to use the swamps, we cut weeks off our circuit—including all the stretches when we do nothing but travel."

"I rather like those," said Wiltwain.

"Think of it, Master Overseer," said Rombol. "We'll make enough to retire ten years before we'd planned."

Wiltwain had no answer for that but made an appreciative sound.

"So tonight we head straight across for Windwall, where they replace their lost teeth with gold ones."

The Overseer sighed. "The Armfolk won't like it. They say—"

"The Armfolk aren't known for ingenuity or ambition. That's why they row all night, and we sleep in soft beds and count our coins." A smile crept into Rombol's voice. "Have I been wrong before?"

"No, Master and friend—that you have not."

"Nor am I wrong about Weepwallow. The Lady will keep us safer in her land than the King ever has in his. See to the preparations."

Cymbril heard them thump each other's shoulders, and the wagon jerked again. Wiltwain's quick tread hurried away, followed a moment later by Rombol's ponderous steps.

Weepwallow. Urrt and the other Strongarms always fell oddly silent at the mention of its name. Cymbril felt a prickle of dread, but also a thrill of excitement. A part of her was eager to know what lurked among those shadowy trees. Brigit had said: "My Lady of the Wild grants you favor." With the Urrmsh rowing and Loric on the bow, Cymbril didn't see how the Thunder Rake could come to harm.

She also knew, Loric's warning aside, danger or not, that she wasn't going to stay put in her bunk.

Chapter 14

Weepwallow

Throughout the afternoon, Cymbril's gaze strayed toward the drab valley spreading below, the air above it crossed at times by heavy-looking crows. Some of the dead trees at the nearer edge had hardened and whitened in the sun, resembling stacks of bones. As the sun sank lower, a weird chorus drifted up from the swamp—the dusky, warbling croaks of uncountable frogs. Sometimes a bird shrieked, and once Cymbril thought she heard the yowl of what must be a large feral cat. Several people in the market took notice of the sound, glancing toward the trees. Cymbril didn't see the fat frog that afternoon, but she imagined him crouched among the boulders somewhere nearby, puffing himself up and smiling broadly. To him, such a place must feel like home.

By evening her flower garland had begun to wilt, sooner than she'd hoped. She'd watched crafters press flowers in frames or inside books, later arranging them into pictures made entirely of dried, flattened blooms. Cymbril could try that if she had even one book of her own. But she had no possessions—now that she'd given Runa her two incidentals—except for the two treasures. Her clothes, comb, brush, and even her tooth rag belonged to Rombol (though she doubted he'd ever ask for the tooth rag back). Having no baggage would make it easier to escape. She would wear her plainest homespun dress when she left the Rake. The Master could have his brocaded finery and all the puffed sleeves.

Supper was a rich rabbit stew. Cymbril hardly heard what the other maidservants said over the steaming bowls. She was daydreaming of Gorhyv Glyn and of the noisome dark of Weepwallow.

After helping with her share of the washing up, Cymbril dressed in the clothes she wore for workdays inside the Rake— a soft white blouse and a durable gray skirt with a bodice and shoulder straps. The skirt had three pockets that buttoned closed. Cymbril tucked her treasures into her top pocket and fastened it.

She waited in her windowless chamber, the candle glowing beside her. At last the deck shuddered, and the Rake began to roll. Her hand trembled as she picked up the candle. She had just turned toward the door when someone knocked.

"Who is it?" she asked, her voice a surprised quaver.

The door opened, and Wiltwain peered at her down his long, sharp nose. Mistress Ilda, the head of the maidservants' gallery, stood a few steps behind him.

"Go to sleep now, Cymbril," Wiltwain told her. "We are passing through a dangerous region. Master Rombol has ordered a curfew. No one is to leave quarters tonight— especially not you."

Cymbril felt as if the air had been squeezed out of her. "But—"

"No prowling tonight." Wiltwain searched through the jingling keys at his belt.

He meant to lock her in. In desperation, Cymbril remembered one of Loric's tactics. "But what if I have to go to the relief closet?"

The Overseer hesitated, glancing from Cymbril to Mistress Ilda. Then he snapped open the ring that held the keys and shook one loose. "I'll leave this with you, Ilda," he said.

Mistress Ilda blinked to show that she'd heard him. She rarely spoke or wasted a single movement of her wrinkled hands or face.

"Into bed now," said Wiltwain. "Busy day tomorrow.

Call Mistress if you need anything." He pulled the door shut.

Cymbril sank onto the edge of the bed as the key grated in the lock. *Click.* A silent scream rose inside her, and she threw her pillow against the wall. Outside, the footsteps receded.

Chin in her hands, Cymbril tried to think. She was sure calling Mistress Ilda would get no results. The old woman was selectively deaf. She heard what she wanted to hear and no more. There was no way out of the bunk, and Cymbril would miss the entire journey through Weepwallow. Even worse, if they made a habit of locking her in at night, how could she and Loric ever escape?

She was about to change into her nightdress when a thought struck her. After the lock's *click,* she hadn't heard the key slide out again. She crossed to the door and peeped into the keyhole.

Blackness. The key was still in the lock. That was Mistress Ilda's efficiency—no wasted movement of pocketing the key. In the keyhole, it wouldn't get lost.

Crouching beside the door, Cymbril set down the candle and listened for a long time. There were no sounds in the hallway. She hurried to her trunk and took out her dark hooded rain cloak. Carefully she unfolded it and, starting with a corner, slid the hem through the crack under her door. The stiff cloth went smoothly, and she pushed it with her fingers, little by little, until more than half of it lay spread across the planks outside her chamber. Then she unbuttoned her pocket and withdrew the jeweled hairpin. Holding her breath, she pushed the long, skinny end into the keyhole—a perfect fit. When it touched something hard, something that blocked its progress, she gently wiggled it and pushed a little harder.

Clunk!

The key fell onto the cloak outside. Now, if only it had not bounced away . . . if only it would fit beneath the door. Slowly, she pulled the cloak back—and the key came with it!

Cymbril whirled to the trunk again. She gathered an armload of dresses and arranged them under the bedcovers in a shape that looked like her. Putting on the cloak, she tucked her hair away, pulling the hood low around her face. Then she used the key to unlock the door.

She opened it a crack. No one was in the hall, but the night lantern flickered at the bend, giving enough light to see by. Cymbril put her candle onto the bedside stand and blew it out. When she had eased into the corridor, she locked the door and left the key in the lock.

As quietly as her leather slippers would carry her, she made her way into the Rake's deep darkness.

At the mouth of the Ferny Way on the top deck, she almost blundered in front of an armored guard who stood like a statue, leaning on his halberd. The hallways and decks were deserted. Doors normally left open were closed. More torches than usual burned on poles along the deck, driving back shadows. Cymbril had to change her route three times and wriggle behind a row of potted rosebushes.

A few cats were about tonight, slinking around corners and under hedges. Cymbril stopped to pet the friendlier ones. She saw no sign of Miwa.

Overhead, a ceiling of limbs closed across the thin moon. Cymbril had never seen trees taller than the Rake. In fact, she'd wondered where its builders had found even the trunks for the craft's arms, which would only reach from the ground to the lowest rail if stood on end. What had looked like dwarf trees from Ardle's ridge were unthinkably enormous when seen from the swamp itself, black towers that leaned over the passing city wagon like nosy giants.

Cymbril didn't hurry toward the bow. She edged among horse barns to the left rail, where the torches were widely spaced. She liked the scent of the horses, their gentle sighs, the occasional soft stamp of a hoof, and the contented munching from one still awake. She had always marveled at the way horses slept standing up. That was true readiness, it seemed to her.

Below the rail, the Rake's claws rammed through clumps of bushes. Something black and glistening flew in circles around a torch, wings beating with a *thwick-thwick-thwick*. Though the Rake followed the driest ground, it also had to avoid the trees. Often a wheel sagged into a squishy hole and the decks tilted so steeply that cargo rumbled in the holds.

Crouching beneath a windlass at the rail, Cymbril listened to a guard's footsteps passing on a balcony above. Out across the swamp, balls of eerie fire rose from the water near and far, pale pink, green, and yellow. She watched the fiery globes floating among the roots, bobbing, appearing to spin. They seemed almost alive, fairies or sprites of Weepwallow.

As her gaze swept across a hillock between far-off trunks, Cymbril gasped. When she blinked, the image was gone— but for the briefest instant, she was certain she'd seen someone on horseback, a rider watching from the swamp, cloaked and still in the half-light. The rider's long hair draped her shoulders, unbound and shimmering. *Wildhair.* Cymbril's pulse thudded in her throat. *The Lady is watching.* The glimpse brought a thrill that was more excitement than dread.

Cymbril couldn't reach the crank basket down to her secret hatchway in the prow—too many guards. Why were the soldiers out? Hadn't Rombol said that the Rake would be safe in Wildhair's country? Did the Master expect a battle with the trees? The thought wasn't funny. It was easy to imagine grotesque faces on the mossy trunks.

From the winery's roof, she'd have a perfect view. When the Rake began to splash through shallow water, Cymbril climbed a lattice grape arbor. Wriggling up onto the gambrel, she wondered if perhaps she'd carried this idea too far. Vines from the swamp's trees dragged past her, dropping moldy leaves and tiny multi-legged shapes that skittered in all directions. Alone on the roof, she felt unprotected beneath the rotting, breathing ceiling of Weepwallow. Just a look around, and then she'd go down to a safer hiding place.

A raised middle section of the roof screened her from the view of anyone in the higher wheelhouse. She rolled to one side, letting a vine slither past, and then crawled forward. Pairs of eyes glinted from forks and holes in the trees. Aside from the cold-looking marsh fires, all the rest was blackness. Loric must be busy indeed tonight.

Could the Huntress see in the dark, like a Fey? Could she see Cymbril crawling on the roof?

Cymbril saw Loric first, dressed in the patched tunic and trousers. As her chin cleared the roof's edge, she spied

Rombol, Wiltwain, and about ten men-at-arms. She pulled her head back quickly before any of them looked up.

Sliding the stone from her pocket, she cupped it in both hands to hide its light and touched it to her forehead. *Loric? Can you hear me?*

I hear you, Cymbril.

Cymbril felt a surge of happiness just to hear his voice again. The strength of the emotion surprised her.

You shouldn't be here, he said. *Especially not on the open roof. There are things in the trees. Things everywhere. Rombol shouldn't have brought us this way. There's danger—*He interrupted himself to call a direction to the pilot about a deadfall of limbs and trunks ahead concealing what might be a deep hole under the water. The Rake circled it on the left, trundling off an earth bank at such a pitch that Cymbril flattened herself to keep from sliding. The men yelled and grabbed the rails. In a draft, the torches flared sideways.

Things in the trees. Breathing shakily, Cymbril shot her gaze from one leafy hollow to the next, flinching at each hint of sound, each furtive movement. A wayward strand of hair kept falling across her eyes, blocking her view.

When she could raise her hands to her brow again, she asked, *What danger?*

All this noise we make, he said. *Wheels turning, claws*

gouging. Old and terrible things sleep here, things that ought not to be disturbed.

"The ground is too soft," Wiltwain said. "The claws are sifting it, not pulling us forward."

"We need momentum," said Rombol. "Tell the Arm-folk to row harder."

Wiltwain blew a signal on his shell trumpet, its tone ringing away among the trees. The Rake's arms cycled faster.

"No," said Loric, sounding afraid.

Cymbril raised her head. He was speaking aloud the same words he was thinking, his voice shrill. It was unsettling to hear the same words with her ears and in her mind. But she kept the Star Shard against her forehead, fearful of missing any thought.

"The night's ear hears us," Loric gasped, backing as far from the bow as his chain would stretch. "The night's eye sees us. We're like field mice to a hawk."

"Keep *your* eyes open, boy!" Rombol shoved him forward.

Leaves shivered, the laughter, the whispers of the trees. Gnarled and burled, the trees loomed more densely, pressing closer. And between their slick, fungous trunks, darkness swirled. Even the wet leaves of the undergrowth, reflecting the Rake's lamps, faded from view. It was as if the darkness were more than an absence of light. Rather, it seemed a heavy coldness that *swallowed* light, pulling all shapes into oblivion.

"Something's coming." Loric dropped to his knees, his arms up to shield his head. "It's coming! It's HERE!"

Rombol bellowed an order, but his words were drowned by a shriek that pierced Cymbril like an icy wind.

Her heart hammered. Clutching the Star Shard against her, she whipped around, looking for what had screamed. It had been louder than any human voice.

The cry echoed again, and with it came a slow flapping of wings. A shape swooped over the Rake, much too large to be a bird. The dismal screech tore from it as it passed, and Cymbril caught a foul smell, worse than waste pits.

Men raised pole arms or drew swords. Loric cringed against the rail, his ears covered, knees pulled to his chin. In the barns behind the winery, the horses whinnied in terror, thumping their plank walls.

Cymbril pushed the stone into her pocket and squirmed for a clearer view.

"Get under cover!" Loric yelled.

The flying thing perched on a tree limb, its wings flung wide. Torch light shone on brown feathers mottled with black.

The body was as broad as a bull's, its sharp talons as large as an Armfolk's hand. When Cymbril saw the face, she could not hold back a whimper.

The head was not a bird's, but that of an ancient woman. Gray hair jutted in filthy spikes. A cruel mouth turned down at the corners. Lips peeled back from jagged teeth in black gums, and the hag-monster shrieked again, its eyes fixed on Cymbril.

"A harpy!" shouted Wiltwain, cuffing the shoulders of the guards. "Stand ready!"

Cymbril had heard tales of harpies, but no words had prepared her.

The harpy ignored the knot of men. Wings pumping the night air, it launched itself toward Cymbril. The eyes bored into hers, and Cymbril felt frozen in place.

"Cymbril!"

Loric's cry pulled her gaze away from the monster's, breaking its spell. As the claws uncurled, reaching for her, Cymbril threw herself to the right. The talons narrowly missed her, tearing instead into the boards, planing up ribbons of wood. Banking left over the aft towers, the harpy screamed in anger.

Cymbril heard the wing beats returning. The harpy

would not miss a second time. It swooped above the orchards, above the dining hall, gaining speed.

Loric leaped to his feet. "Cymbril," he cried, "jump!"

Cymbril sensed the hideous face behind her, the yellow teeth. She snatched a double handful of her skirt to free her ankles and lurched forward, barely staying upright. As she sprinted to the roof's edge, harsh screams shook the planks.

It was a long fall to the bow, but she couldn't hesitate. She picked the biggest target—Rombol—and dove into space.

Chapter 15

The Nightmare

The guards tipped their halberds aside as she flew toward them. She felt a tug at her neck and the ripping of cloth. Rombol caught and spun her, lessening the impact. Her face sank into his bristly beard.

Rombol dropped with her to the deck. The harpy soared so close above that tail feathers brushed their backs. Its claws had shredded Cymbril's cloak down to the hem.

The beast made a lunge for Loric.

He threw himself flat.

The harpy pulled up to avoid the rail, and its grasp missed Loric. But one talon closed on the chain that held him, just where the manacle encircled the post. The rail shattered, and the post jerked free. Still clutching the chain, the harpy crowed in triumph and winged upward.

Loric had the presence of mind to grab the chain in both hands, taking the snap of force in his arms when the chain sprang taut. He was snatched off the deck and swung through the air below the flapping creature.

Rombol roared.

The harpy, eyes forward again, saw a mighty tree looming just ahead and rolled wildly to the left. But the arcing chain looped across the bark, yanking the shackle from the monster's grip. Loric passed the tree on the right.

He circled behind the trunk as the chain wrapped around it like a Maypole ribbon. Loric smacked against the tree and went limp.

Beyond, the harpy swooped among shadowy limbs, circling back.

The deck tipped forward. Guards staggered.

No one had told the helmsman to turn. No one had told the Armfolk to stop rowing. The Rake nosed over the brink of a steep incline.

"Stop! Stop!" men shouted. Wiltwain fumbled for his trumpet shell. The Rake's arms clawed at empty air. Groaning, the craft rode its axle.

Cymbril tumbled to the rail and searched for Loric.

He hung against the tree, head lolling. His chain loosened, unwinding, and he was sliding slowly down the bark. Too slowly—the Rake's bow plunged, driven by the weight of the decks and all their cargo. When it hit the tree, it would smash Loric.

Again Cymbril had no time to think. She couldn't see the ground or the harpy. All she saw was Loric, stunned, hanging from his iron collar.

Rombol bounded toward her, but he caught no more than a tatter of her cloak as she vaulted over the rail.

She hadn't far to jump. The inclining bow had almost reached the tree. With Wiltwain's horn sounding in her ears, Cymbril caught Loric, her knees scraping painfully against the trunk. Arms around him, she rolled on her left shoulder, following the chain.

The chain snagged on bark, holding them for a dangling, dizzy moment on the trunk's far side. The Rake struck. Vibrations passed through the wood, and every branch Cymbril could see separated for an instant into multiple ghost-images of itself, all wavering. A splintering *crack* traveled up from deep below, as if the Earth itself had broken a bone. Birds squawked from a knothole. Chunks of moss pattered among hairy vines. The tree tilted.

Her back against the trunk, Cymbril did not let herself consider how high above the ground they must be. She looked over Loric's shoulder—into the glowering face of the harpy.

The monster sped toward them out of the darkness, its shriveled features a mask of hunger. Loric stirred, his hair drifting across Cymbril's face. There was no escape this time. They swung outward as the tree leaned. The chain loosened again, slithering off the bark, and they slid with it. The harpy's lips pulled back in a wicked smile.

Above their heads, the stump of a dead, broken limb jutted out from the trunk, its angle changing with the tree's slow fall. The harpy, intent on its prey, flew headlong into this blunt, stone-hard lance. With a deafening scream, the monster crunched to a dead stop. Brown feathers swirled in all directions. Its face contorted in agony, and the harpy tumbled backwards, wings flopping.

Cymbril and Loric were falling, too. The colossal tree toppled with them, crashing through other limbs. Her arm around Loric, Cymbril gripped the chain. The tree swung them forward, dank wind whistling in their ears, and the last metal links snaked free of the trunk.

Bushes on a steep slope hurtled up to meet them. Cymbril's feet furrowed through their branches. Suddenly she and Loric were tumbling heels over heads, lashed by shrubs, scratched by twigs—but cushioned by deep moss, as if they were falling down a staircase of pillows.

Snapping booms rolled above like thunder. The air rained dirt and dead leaves. Seeds and pebbles bounced over Cymbril's head, and some vast, dark shape lowered like a ceiling. She landed face-down in the moss, her breath knocked out of her.

Slowly, the sounds faded. The ground trembled and lay still. Her face against the moist, velvety moss, Cymbril coughed and inhaled. The smell of earth and mold was overwhelming. She tasted grit.

Loric's eyes, so close to hers she saw nothing else, blinked several times. His chain jingled, and he sat up, sliding from her arms. "Are you all right?" he asked.

Her lips moved before she could force her voice out. "I think so."

She looked up. The tree lay beside them like a cliff, near enough to touch. Ferns and shrubs had been scooped, roots and all, from the soil and lay strewn in deep piles everywhere. Overhead, just visible in the dimness, the Rake's prow loomed like a wooden sky. Only the trunk had held it off her and Loric. A gigantic tree limb had embedded itself just at their feet. Loric leaned against it to struggle upright. Tree, prow, and piercing limb—any of the three might easily have crushed them.

Cymbril kept still, listening, hardly daring to breathe. Where was the harpy?

"It's gone," Loric whispered, seeing her worry. "I don't sense it anywhere nearby. It was injured."

Shouts came from high above, men calling for Cymbril and Loric. Torch light glimmered from the bow.

Loric smiled at her, pulling in the loose chain hand over hand, coiling it around his wrist. "I'll thank you soon for saving my life," he said. "But first, we have to run."

Cymbril drew a wondering breath. They wouldn't be needing the key after all—they were free. With Loric's sight, they could easily elude the soldiers in the swamp.

"It's a long way," said Loric, "but we can reach Gorhyv Glyn. Are you ready?"

Cymbril patted her pocket. The stone and the hairpin were there. She was ready. Laughing, she took Loric's hand.

But she couldn't stand up. It was as if the ground wouldn't let her go. Pulling up the hem of her skirt, she saw her left leg was caught beneath the tree limb, deep in the mud. She could wiggle her toes and foot—the mire had saved her from being hurt, but a fork of the limb rested squarely on her lower leg. No matter how she pulled and twisted, she couldn't free herself.

Loric dug with his fingers, scooping out armloads of

muck, his shirt and trousers black with it. But when he made a little progress, the limb settled lower. The weight on her leg increased, scaring Cymbril. She braced her other foot and strained until the wood gouged her shin, but it was no use. Tears welled in her eyes. She pounded her hands against the bark.

"All right," said Loric with a sigh, sitting down in the moss. "Don't hurt yourself."

Cymbril sagged back, gasping, and clenched her fists. "You have to go," she said. Even now, Rombol's men would be racing down ladders, pouring from the bottom hatches.

Loric smiled again and squeezed her wrist. "When we go," he said, "we'll go together."

Now Cymbril couldn't hold back the tears.

With a sudden, nervous flicker in his gaze, Loric leaned close and quickly kissed the side of her head.

As she turned a wide-eyed glance upon him, he hurried out into the brightening torch light. "We're safe," he called, facing the sound of footsteps. "But we need a shovel."

Digging Cymbril free was the easy part. It took the rest of the night to get the Rake back on level ground. The vessel wasn't built to crawl backwards, so the claws were useless. Since the slope below was blocked by close-set, tremendous trees and then a bog, the Armfolk had to hoist the city wagon up to the ridge again. The movements of the Urrmsh were purposeful and unfailingly effective, but slow as the turning of seasons. An hour slipped by as they simply got into position. They wrapped chains around trees and carried boulders to brace the wheels. All the while Rombol fumed and gave orders, unable to blame anyone but himself. Before the Rake could resume its journey, the Urrmsh needed to splint a claw arm that had fractured.

The Huntress might have been watching, and Rombol might have had her favor, but he certainly did not receive her help—unless she was holding back the wild beasts of her domain. Certain night birds gave the impression of cackling, mocking the intruders and their silly wooden monstrosity.

The soldiers stood guard, waving firebrands at glowing eyes that drifted nearer, some disturbingly large and high above the ground, increasing in number on every side. A hunting party of the bravest men ventured a few paces into the trees, but the harpy had vanished—which made Rombol all the angrier: he'd hoped to put the creature into a cage. The search for the winged hag ended abruptly when one of the men saw a huge, snarling shadow that frightened him so badly he could not describe it—nearly as anyone could guess, it had been a gigantic wolf.

Cymbril heard all this later from Urrt. She and Loric were sent inside the Rake, allowed to wash, and after a healer tended her, Cymbril was put to bed. Her only wounds were skinned patches on her knees and shins, and a few scratches from thorns. She was thankful she still had both legs.

Over and over, she thought of Loric's quick, impulsive little kiss, his face and clothes covered with mud. He had stayed. He had stayed in captivity because Cymbril couldn't go with him. The thought made her insides feel light and watery.

The baying of wolves reached Cymbril in her chamber, raising goose flesh on her arms. If she and Loric had escaped, they would be out there now with the hungry pack on their trail. No wolf would attack the Armfolk, so she did not fear for them. With the Urrmsh heaving and towing all around the wagon city, she felt safe in her warm bunk, but she ached with a bitter disappointment. For one moment, she had known the joy of freedom. She had pictured herself running beside Loric, careening over roots, and following the paths of wild things, the wind streaming in her hair. They'd been outside the Rake, alone in the night, with no walls to hold them in. But now they were back in the cage, and punishment was sure to come. At last, exhausted as much by regret as by physical exertion, she sank into sleep.

Her dreams were strange and troubling, full of ember eyes and the chorus of the wolves. And always, always she dreamed of a Lady in the shadows, pale eyes aglow, always watching.

Cymbril awoke with a gasp in the blackness. The blanket clung tightly around her, as if she'd been tossing. Her hair stuck to the damp, chilly sweat on her neck. The darkness of her room sat like a weight on her chest. Fighting to loosen the patched cover, she sat up, hands bunched at her throat.

Nightmare. She'd been having a nightmare. There was no dark figure squatting on her chest, crushing away her breath . . . There were no glittering eyes. When she could move again, she dove for her trunk and flung it open, sighing with relief as the mingled light of her two treasures shone from atop her folded clothing. She grasped the hairpin and held up the Star Shard like a lantern. Barefoot, shivering, she peered into the corners and under her bed.

Of course there was no one else here. And yet what had woken her, she felt certain, was the nearness of *something*, some terrible *thing* that was now not quite so near. Raising her head, she glanced at the door. An icy tingle passed over her scalp. Something had been out there, in the hallway. Something had been just on the other side of her door.

The creature that grunted like a pig and breathed in the dark—it was real, and it was still onboard.

The door was no longer locked. Cymbril remembered noticing, in her weary state as she'd come to bed, that the key was where she'd left it, sticking in the keyhole outside. No one had turned it to lock her in again. She took hold of the door's handle, determined to yank the portal open and shine her blue-green light into the corridor. It would be a simple matter to retrieve the key and secure the room.

Yet after a long moment, she backed away from the door and slid into bed, the stone and pin clasped firmly to her chest.

Even for Cymbril, there was a time to let well enough alone.

Chapter 16

The New Evil

In daylight the Rake rolled slowly to Windwall without Loric's guidance. Cymbril helped straighten a larder and several store-rooms where containers had spilled. She was glad for the physical work, which always made the darkness of night seem paler and further away. But all the while, her thoughts were of Loric. Was he all right after the ordeal? He'd come so close to death—or whatever unspeakable fate the harpy had planned.

She thought back through the night's harrowing events. The winged hag's attention had alighted first upon Cymbril. Failing to snatch her from the roof, the monster had seized Loric's chain. *I suppose we looked more tender than the soldiers and Rombol,* Cymbril thought with a shiver, *and we were light enough to carry.*

Over and over, she let herself recall the shy, swift press of Loric's lips against her hair. The memory brought a feeling like a tiny bird beating its wings inside her chest, a tickling thrill. He might have escaped, but he'd stayed for her. What she'd learned about him in that moment was a treasure she carried now, like the stone and pin from her parents, secret and safe. No matter what was happening around her, she could think about Loric and feel that fluttering joy.

First thing in the morning, she'd found Wiltwain and tried to tell him about the presence outside her door. But he was seething with tension, dealing with Rombol's mood and responsible for a hundred tasks in putting the Rake to rights. "A nightmare," he said, patting her shoulders. "You saw a harpy in the flesh. Be glad you came away with nothing more than nightmares."

About to resume his duties, he stopped and narrowed his eyes at her.

Cymbril drew a breath. She'd been temporarily forgotten in the hubbub, but now the reckoning would surely come.

"You used magic, didn't you?" Wiltwain stared at her, and she couldn't decide whether he was angry or amazed. "You're as witchy as that Fey boy. It's the only way I can imagine that you got out of a locked room."

"I—I used my hairpin," she stammered—which was true, only not in the way that Wiltwain seemed to think.

"I knew it!" He frowned, apparently at a loss, and then rubbed his temples wearily. "The Master is too furious at all this to deal with you today." He swept his hand in a gesture that must mean the swamp and the Rake. "So he's turned your punishment over to me. I can't lock you up. I can't take away your enchanted pin. What would you suggest, Cymbril? What would you do with you, if you were me?"

"I—" Cymbril blinked and shrugged. She wasn't about to help him think of ways to punish her.

A merchant signaled to Wiltwain, calling him to examine a shattered pulley.

"I'll think on it," the Overseer said to Cymbril. "Meanwhile, you can start by lending a hand today along with the other maidservants from your block. Let's just try to get out of this mud hole in one piece."

Later, in the storeroom where Cymbril was reshelving tins, Miwa found her and rubbed against her ankles, asking to be petted. "What's aboard this Rake, Miwa?" Cymbril whispered in her ear. "If you can't tell me, then tell Loric." Feeling jumpy in the darker galleries, Cymbril was glad at first even for the company of the other girls, with their boorish gossip and talk of boys—though today their topics were mostly of last night's fright, the crash of the Rake that had flung everyone out of bed, and the rumors of the winged monster, which became—for those who had not seen it—a fanged woman with serpents for hair, whose gaze had turned two men-at-arms into stone.

"I heard there's another monster," Cymbril ventured. "One that prowls around the corridors at night."

"You mean Bale," said Theriel with a lopsided grin. "He's a dog."

"No, something else," Cymbril insisted. "Something worse than Bale."

Briella, the block leader, gave her a withering look. "Everyone knows about *that* monster. It's been around for weeks."

Three other girls perked up their ears, the brushes and rags in their hands slowing down.

Briella lowered her voice. "The two old witches with the frog made it on a table, from the skin of a dead horse. They put sheep guts and magic herbs and a human heart inside—still beating—and sewed up the skin."

"Whose heart was it?" asked a girl named Tansy.

Now Briella clucked her tongue at Tansy's ignorance. "In every city, the witches have a secret contract with the captain of the guard. In the middle-night, the frog hops into the jail, where they keep the convicted prisoners waiting for the headsman's ax. The frog takes along a bag of gold, dragging it with the cord in his icky mouth. When he hops back out, the bag is full of warm hearts that the witches use in their spells."

"Why did they make the monster?" asked Jen, who looked skeptical but amused.

Briella spoke in such a hush that they all had to lean closer. "It's looking for the person who cheated the witches out of one copper coin. When it finds him . . ." Briella widened her eyes ominously.

So no one had seen or heard the creature that really lurked onboard.

Cymbril threw herself into the work, remembering the days before she'd been the Thrush of the Rake, when—aside from voice lessons—there had been endless carrying, dusting, polishing, and scrubbing of floors, even though she'd been very young. She sighed. By removing her from the drudgery, by setting her upon a perch to sing, Rombol had guaranteed she would have no human friends. Who wanted to be friends with an ornament?

All day she longed to curl up in the warmth beneath a rowing bench and listen to the songs of the Urrmsh. But the

Rake had endured such a shaking that she was kept busy until suppertime.

There were no further mishaps under the bearded trees, but it was evening by the time Rombol's Rake, plastered with mud, crawled like a defeated beast up the last slope beneath the high, meandering stone wall of the city. Rombol called a halt beside a stream, and his men did nothing more that night than wash the wheels, axles, arms, and underside of the Rake. They dumped bucket after bucket of muddy water back down the rocky gully.

When at last Cymbril found her way to the footboards beside Urrt, most of the Strongarms had disembarked to help with the washing and to sleep outdoors like great boulders in the dark. Urrt and his bench-mate Arrubh were too tired to be of much help. The third time Urrt's eyelids drooped closed, Cymbril realized just what a tremendous labor it had been to rescue the Rake. In a single night, the Urrmsh had accomplished a task that would have confounded a human army. Then they had rowed throughout the day.

Even so, the Urrmsh did their best to listen sympathetically.

She told them about the nightly noises—the snorting creature that Bale had been barking at since before Weepwallow—and how she was certain it had been outside her door during the night. And deciding she'd better give them all the details she could, she confessed that she'd been to the Night Market.

Urrt and Arrubh looked down at her with wide eyes.

She did her best to explain. "I went there to buy a skeleton key for Loric's collar and the Nixielixir that made Gerta and Berta beautiful. Only I didn't have enough money, so the Eye Women took back the skeleton key as the exacted difference." She told of encountering Brigit, too, and of how Brigit had known Cymbril's name and said, "You've grown."

Both Urrmsh gazed at her in amazement. Urrt looked around the nearly deserted Pushpull Chamber, apparently checking for eavesdroppers. Leaning forward, he spoke in a quiet rumble. "When you saw this woman Brigit, what was she doing?"

"She was . . ." Cymbril sprang up onto her knees and gripped the edge of the bench, remembering the cloaked men with Brigit. There'd been a wagon, a cage on wheels wrapped around with heavy chains.

"She was bringing the monster onboard."

Cymbril didn't leave her room that night. Instead, she rested and tried to think of ways to get the key for Loric's collar. The rescue, she supposed, would have to be done under the cover of darkness. But it would have to be a night on which Loric wasn't guiding the Rake.

She wished it were easier to talk to him whenever she wanted. He would have better ideas about how to manage things. With a sigh, she took out her two treasures and tried again to call out to Loric through the Star Shard. But his chamber was too far away. Once more she imagined her parents, her mother with shining hair, her father a taller version of Loric— lean and mysterious, with clothes that seemed cut from the sea and the night. If only she had even one clear memory . . .

She hoped the snorting monster wouldn't come again to her door.

At last she blew out her candle and slept.

All during the market day at Windwall, piles of gray clouds threatened rain, as if Rombol's mood affected nature itself. Today he'd left his goose-headed stick indoors, and his morning speech in the ramp chamber was only a glance around and a nod.

Windwall was a stone fortress-city on a stone ridge, altogether as gray as the sky. The Rake crouched against the crenelated wall like the siege engine of an invading army, the ramp leading straight down through an open side gate. There was no soil to warm and soften the footing, no greenery to sweeten the air. In this outpost of the King's troops, even the women seemed to march as they moved through the market, towing their quiet children. The Armfolk had no woodland to retreat to, so they also spent the day in the garrison square. Cymbril knew the Urrmsh were secretly hoping the sky might deliver rain. Wet weather was unfavorable for the merchants, but the Strongarms enjoyed a good drizzle as much as they loved shadowed streams in forest glens.

Cymbril thought her own voice sounded pinched and feeble, half drowned by the wind against the battlements. Still, people made their requests, pressing close to see her. They smiled and clapped as she finished each song. Watching the gray sky, Cymbril pondered again how close she and Loric had come to freedom. The barrenness of the stone city made her all the more conscious of the cage she lived in. *I need the forest,* she thought. *I need to see my father's homeland. My chains aren't visible like Loric's, but if I don't get free of them, I'll die.*

On a sudden impulse, she ignored the requests that people were calling and launched into a song of her own choosing. Throwing back her shoulders, she lifted her face to the wind

and sang "The Green Leaves of Eireigh" with such passion
that the crowd stood transfixed.

> *The green leaves of Eireigh when summer is there,*
> *Aglow in the sunlight, are laughing and fair;*
> *With memory's whisper they call as I roam:*
> *"Come, wanderer, back to the forests of home.*
> *Come back to the wildwood, the forests of home.*
>
> *"The roads of the lowland are weary and long,*
> *So far from warm shadows that echo with song.*
> *In Eireigh's soft twilight the hearth fires burn,*
> *Awaiting the wayworn, the lost one's return;*
> *Come back to the greenwood; to Eireigh return."*
>
> *My heart is still there in the misty blue hills,*
> *Where the glens are a-sparkle with chattering rills,*
> *And the oaks cluster dark on the shoulders of stone.*
> *I'll take up my pack and journey alone;*
> *I'll pray for what's needful and journey alone.*
>
> *A strong bow of yew and boots of good leather,*
> *A kindness of sun, the wind in the heather,*
> *A jerkin of green and a mantle of gray,*

And a steed to carry me far and away,
A steed to carry me back to Eireigh.

When she'd finished, at first there was a hush broken only by the wind moaning past the towers. Then there was a collective sigh as the music's spell lifted. The applause began, and the captain of the city guard led his men in a cheer. The Urrmsh joined them with voices like deep horns, and the cheer rolled on and on, echoing from the walls.

The Urrmsh were especially popular with the soldiers, who never seemed to tire of watching them hurl boulders and tug teams of men across lines. In exchange for these displays, the men dropped bright coins into the sacks at the Strong-arms' feet.

Wiltwain came by on his rounds, looking tired. "Rest awhile," he told Cymbril. Brushing his long hair back with his fingers, he braced a foot on the wagon and leaned on his raised knee. "Quite a rousing rendition of 'Eireigh,'" he said, not quite smiling. "I don't think I've ever heard you sing it that well. Where did you learn it?"

Cymbril sat in the wagon bed. "It was one of the first Mistress Selene taught me when I was young."

Wiltwain laughed, expelling air through his nose. "When you were young. Yes, all those years ago."

"People in the western towns request it often," Cymbril said. "There are other versions. I heard one where the singer goes home at the end, actually reaches Eireigh, but I can't remember the words."

Wiltwain stretched his back. "Do you know where Eireigh is?"

Cymbril shook her head. It was nowhere the Rake ever went. She'd always supposed it was a made-up place, existing only in the song.

"If you believe the old stories," Wiltwain said, "it's a part of the Fey lands, where those like Loric come from. So the person singing the song is Fey." He watched her with an eyebrow raised.

"Oh," said Cymbril.

The Overseer stepped back and hooked his thumbs into his belt. "In the swamp, we all thought the harpy had gotten you."

"She almost did. We almost died."

"In at least four different ways—I'm glad you realize that. Cats have nine lives. Little girls have one. Even girls with magic stones, as far as I know." Wiltwain spread his palm on the top of her head. "For now, your tablet is clean. You broke the curfew, but you also saved the elf boy's life. That was brave. Brave, goodhearted, and very foolish."

"Well," said Cymbril, "that's two good things out of three."

Wiltwain eyed her darkly, squinted at the clouds, and strode off.

A few drops of rain fell. Cymbril put on her torn rain cloak but left the hood down. Although the sky rumbled, it wasn't truly raining yet. She smiled across the cobbles at Urrt.

After her next song, Cymbril glimpsed the fat frog hopping through the market's open center, gazing appreciatively at the gloomy sky and glaring at the customers who stepped around him, distaste in their faces. Cymbril wondered why Rombol put up with the frog. He was nothing if not bad for business. She could only conclude that the Master was afraid of the Eye Women. She doubted he'd even questioned them about the Night Market.

For all his wealth and power, there were people Rombol feared: those old sisters, Brigit, and certainly the Lady of the Wild herself. The women in his life frightened him, Cymbril thought with a smile—especially the ones he could not understand or clap into a cage.

———

That evening, when Cymbril managed to linger near Loric's door, he warned her that they would need the key soon. He'd been asking Miwa about the Rake's route and schedule, which the cat remembered well. Also, Miwa had had a recent peek at Rombol's map. In three days the Rake would hold a market in Berryholt, a town above a wooded ravine called the Green-mouth—which was the entrance to Gorhyv Glyn.

Berryholt is small, said Loric in Cymbril's mind. *I'm sure we'll only be there one day. The best time for escape will be just before dawn on the morning we arrive, after I'm brought back to my room. With any luck, Master Rombol will be in bed.*

If we wait too long, said Cymbril, *he'll be up and getting ready.*

Yes. It will have to be precisely timed. When I'm on the bow, Rombol leaves the key with the guards. If we reach the destination before sunrise, the guards lock me into my room and slide the key under Rombol's door.

Cymbril jumped at a scratching sound. But it came from Loric's room—or more precisely, from his threshold. Through the crack beneath the door, he was pushing out a piece of stiff wire as long as Cymbril's forearm.

I found this on the ground in Banburnish and put it up my sleeve. It's been here under my bedroll ever since. It should be just the thing you need.

Cymbril picked up the wire. *For what?*

When the guards leave the key under Rombol's door, you'll be hiding nearby. After they've gone, you can use this to drag the key back out.

Cymbril's heart beat faster. *Perfect!*

Hardly perfect. Too much could go wrong. But it's a chance.

And what about the . . . the thing that walks around at night? she asked.

Miwa's had a glimpse of it. From what she describes, it sounds like a black nargus.

Cymbril had no idea what a black nargus might be. *I think Brigit brought it aboard at the Night Market,* she said.

That fits, said Loric. *A nargus is a magic-sniffer. That's why it came to the prow when we were using the Star Shard to talk—and why it's likely to come nosing around your bunk, so keep your door closed tight. It can smell anything enchanted.*

It smells my stone and hairpin?

Yes, but don't worry. Its nose tells the nargus that they're not what it's really looking for. I think the Eye Women bought the nargus from Brigit because of the magic storerooms you found. They suspect there are a lot more vaults or cupboards on this Rake, a lot more hidden magical treasures. They mean to find more—that's likely the reason they travel with Master Rombol.

Cymbril fingered the Star Shard. *We're using magic now,* she thought.

Yes, but it's early. The nargus comes out when the Rake is quiet.

Is it dangerous?

I would guess the Sisters aren't feeding it. The hungrier it gets, the sharper its sense of smell. But a hungry nargus is very unstable. They're bad-tempered at best. When they're starving . . . My people have an expression: "A moth's draft to a nargus"—it means a little thing, like the puff of breeze from a moth's wings, that sets off the fury of a storm.

Chapter 17

Restless

For the next two days, Cymbril's thoughts whirled like a spring wind, going in one direction, then in another, full of restless hope and anxiety. As much as she despised the constraints of the Rake, it had been home for almost as long as she could remember. Now that she would be leaving, she could hardly bear to walk in the mossy alleys, to climb the ladders of half-levels, and to ride the crank baskets. Never to pass the Candleway again . . . never to skulk through the shadows of Longwander . . . At breakfast Miwa rubbed her ankles, and Cymbril felt a pain at the base of her throat. She held the cat on her lap for a long time, stroking Miwa's silvery fur. "I don't think you can come with me this time," Cymbril whispered to her old friend. Miwa wasn't hers to take along. Probably the forest home of the Sidhe was no place for a cat, anyway. Yet Miwa had been around for so long—always helpful, always seeming to understand what Cymbril felt, what she needed. Cymbril rubbed her face on Miwa's silky head.

And of course Cymbril would miss Urrt and the other Urrmsh. How could she say goodbye to them?

Even the Rake's grand circuit tugged at her heart: the cities and towns under the changing seasons, each far-flung wall built of different stones, the morning light different on each thatch, the breath of each hay field different in sweetness. It was her enslavement that had allowed her to see so much of the world. She thought of the seas of human faces. *I'll be out among them,* she reminded herself. *When I'm free, the whole world will be spread out before me and waiting.*

The necklace of swamp flowers was withered now. She'd hung it on a cloak peg. The dry garland broke beneath her fingers, the petals swirling to the floor. She knelt and sifted through the dead blossoms, thinking of Gorhyv Glyn and what it might be like there. Would she be happier? Would the Sidhe accept her as one of their own? It was hard to abandon the comfort of a home she could see around her in search of one that was still unknown. Change took courage, but leaving the Rake was a change she needed, beyond the fears and the pain. Deep down, Cymbril knew she needed to be free.

Not long before, she'd watched a gardener on the top deck transplanting rosebushes from clay pots into deeper soil beds. When they came out of the pots, the roots were bunched up in cramped tangles. Cymbril almost believed she could hear the plants sighing with relief when the gardener settled them into the black earth, where they could stretch like sleepers awakening. *I'm like the roses,* Cymbril thought. Huge as the Rake was, it was still a very tight clay pot.

After the next day of work in Blue Barrows, she went to see Urrt. She'd thought of a half-dozen ways to bid him farewell, but she used none of them. Sitting beside his feet, she began to weep.

"Ah," he rumbled, pulling and pushing on the oar. "Yes. We are coming soon to the place you are going, little thrush." Around them, a long, humming tale went on—or maybe it was a song.

Cymbril hugged his knee and shook as waves of agony she'd never expected rolled through her. Tears spilled from her eyes, and her nose ran.

"Little bird." Urrt's palm brushed her hair, gently as the falling of light. "This is a song I've not heard from you before. But it is a good song, too, and makes the world better, not worse."

"I thought it would be easier," Cymbril gasped when she could. "If leaving is right, why does it hurt so much?"

"It's the way with life," said Urrt. "Parts of the world are broken, and there's no fixing them until the End. This kind of hurt means you love. And that, songbird, is a treasure better than a stone or a pin. Have courage." After a long pause, he added, "Remember the hatch. It will be open tomorrow night."

Cymbril told him she thought there was a black nargus aboard the Rake and that the Eye Women were responsible.

Urrt considered this news for a long time.

"If that's what it is," he said at last, "then those old sisters in yellow are growing awfully bold, and there's trouble coming. A nargus has a mind like an empty pit. Those women must be controlling it."

"Will the Armfolk be all right?" she asked.

"We will keep watch," Urrt said. "It may be that Master Rombol will need our help before long."

The help of the Armfolk—did Rombol have any idea how fortunate he was to have Urrt and the others rowing for him? Cymbril closed her eyes and rested in the warm space, the Urrmsh song resonating in the wood, in her bones. The next thing she knew, Urrt was nudging her awake.

"You should go back now," Urrt told her, "before they miss you up there."

Cymbril rubbed her face. It felt stiff with dried tears. She took Urrt's hand. Panic fluttered in her chest.

"Go on," Urrt said. "We will talk again soon, I promise you."

Cymbril hurried to her bunk, afraid to look back.

She tossed through the night, sleeping in snatches, springing awake. Once she sat up at a terrible barking from Bale. Not long afterward, when silence had returned, two soldiers trudged down the hallway past her door. She heard the creak and clink of their armor. "Whatever it is," one muttered to the other, "it clawed through that gate like a swatch o' curtain, and there was nothin' left but feathers. Not hardly nothin' o' the cages *themselves*."

"It's a witchy-wolf, I say," the other guard answered. "That's how it gets away. I saw what one did up in Burl Valley when I was a boy."

Then the soldiers passed beyond hearing.

Cymbril pulled the covers close around herself and lay blinking in the dark.

Over and over she picked up the stone and the hairpin,

the two treasures that no one could take from her. As long as she had these, with their glow of Sidhe fire and magic, she carried a part of her parents. Peering into the Star Shard's depths, she could almost see the faces of her mother and father, hazy as dreams remembered on waking.

She was up before dawn and wriggled into her green dress with embroidered leaves on the cape. Today no one had given her orders for what to wear. Her choice of clothing anticipated Gorhyv Glyn, the woodland realm, but it also celebrated summer—the best dress for her last day on the Rake.

The town was Deepdike, named for the mossy trench that circled it, too wide even for a charging horse to leap across, and four fathoms deep. Wooden footbridges spanned it, strong enough to support normal traffic, but the Thunder Rake could not come across to the market square. Instead, a procession of carts and wagons rolled down the ramp and over the bridges.

Cymbril mustered her best efforts, singing with as much conviction as if all the songs told of her own life's journeys. The ballads brought tears to her listeners' eyes, and the merry songs made them grin. At the end of "Blue Were Her Eyes," she saw an old farmer in the crowd suddenly catch his wife by the arms and kiss her. The woman looked back at him in happy surprise, her own blue eyes sparkling from a wrinkled face like those of the woman in the ballad. Cymbril watched the couple as she sang "Lavender and Primrose." All throughout its lilting verses, they danced together, weaving among the other listeners as if they were on the floor of some grand castle ballroom. Perhaps in their minds, Cymbril thought, that's exactly where they were.

Then something happened that had never happened before. Two minstrels bounded through the crowds, a boy and a girl, both a few scant years older than Cymbril. People laughed and clapped in recognition, thumping the pair on the backs as they passed. Their clothes were patched and of poorer cloth than Cymbril's, but equally green, as if the three had dressed to match. The boy and the girl appeared just as Cymbril began "Home, Lads, Home." From the midst of the audience they played along, their fingers flying over the strings of long-necked instruments that hung by straps from their shoulders. As they pounced right up into the wagon bed, one on each side of her, Cymbril stopped in surprise.

"Keep singing!" said the girl. Her black hair hung in a long ponytail, and a spray of faint freckles dotted her face.

Cymbril forged ahead, and they matched her tune with their own voices, blending into harmony. After her initial bewilderment, Cymbril began to laugh inside, as if she were floating in the sky, sweeping with the birds from cloud to cloud. People in the market began to clap in rhythm, and more linked arms and danced. With three voices intertwined, the long cascade of nonsense syllables at the song's end brought exuberant cheers from the crowd.

The minstrels caught Cymbril's hands and bowed with her. She wanted to collapse and catch her breath, but there was no time—now the requests poured in, and the two paused only to be sure Cymbril knew the next tune.

The sun climbed the sky. Even the merchants came out and stood before their stalls to listen. As the singers huddled together to discuss the words to "Far Green Hills," Rombol clanked goblets with the Patron of Deepdike and cupped his free hand around his mouth to shout, "You're doing far too well! Nobody's buying a thing!" The crowd laughed with him—but turned quickly back to the wagon as the three began singing again.

When they took a short rest, Cymbril laughed at the way the two flopped down as they pleased, arms and legs all askew. She'd been taught to sit before crowds with composure, like a lady.

The dark-haired girl offered Cymbril a hand in greeting, her arm swinging out in a broad gesture like a man's. "I'm Bobbin. You have a beautiful voice."

"Thank you. I'm Cymbril."

"We know," said the boy, clasping Cymbril's hand in turn. "You're famous. I'm Argent." Argent had short white-blond hair and the faint beginnings of a beard. He wore a small silver earring.

"We're cousins," Bobbin explained, dangling her feet off the wagon bed. "We can't stay much longer. We're riding with my uncle to Highcircle. He had an errand here this morning."

Cymbril glanced admiringly at their travel-worn boots, bound up to their knees with leather cords. "You're not from here, then," she said.

"No," said Argent with a chuckle. "We're from out there, the Wild. From everywhere. Like you Rake folk."

"You don't have a home?"

"The grandest home," said Bobbin. "I own thousands and thousands of magnificent towers, shaded with royal canopies. I call them 'trees.'"

The cousins laughed easily, and Cymbril joined them. She'd never envied the highborn ladies at the markets— and certainly not the rich vulture-women of the Rake's teabunks—but she felt envy for these two.

"The Wild is the best home." Argent leaned back on his elbows and gazed at the sky. "We were born there."

Cymbril peered longingly toward the trees.

Argent sprang upright. "Are you ready to sing some more? They're getting impatient!" With a courtly bow, he helped Cymbril to her feet.

Never had Cymbril enjoyed a morning's market so much. She was sorry when, glancing at the sun's position, Bobbin and Argent nodded to each other and squeezed Cymbril's hands again. "That's it," Bobbin said. "We ride."

"It's been a privilege," added Argent.

"My privilege," Cymbril said.

As suddenly as they had appeared, the minstrels hopped down out of the wagon. At a trot, Argent acknowledged the crowds, who applauded. Bobbin's ponytail bounced as she spun and waved. In a blink, they were across the market. They stopped once, however, at the Patron's booth, and a clerk counted coins into their hands.

The folk of Deepdike weren't inclined to let Cymbril eat lunch. They were prodders and hair-feelers, leaning too close and breathing on her. Wiltwain rescued her, leading her into the bread baker's tent and settling her onto a stool behind a curtain, handing her a tray of hot bannock and blueberry jam.

As he turned to go, Cymbril spoke quickly. This might be her last chance to say anything to him. "Overseer—did you believe me . . . about the Night Market?"

He lowered his voice. "Master Rombol ordered you not to speak of that again."

"But do you believe me?"

He studied her at length, then nodded.

"You do! Why?"

"Do you suppose yours is the only word we have on it?"

This came as a surprise to Cymbril. But Wiltwain was again preparing to leave, so she plunged ahead. "And do you know that the two old women with the frog bought a black nargus from Brigit?"

He lowered his brows. "What are you talking about?"

"They're looking for more magic, like the things in the storerooms I found. The monster that makes Bale bark at night is a nargus, which sniffs out magic. It will soon be very dangerous, because it's getting hungry. I saw Brigit at the Night Market. She had something inside a box on wheels, all bound up with ropes and chains—probably the nargus, though I can't prove it."

He regarded her dubiously, probably wondering if this were all some flight of her imagination.

"Ask the Armfolk," she said. She knew he respected the Urrmsh. At least he was warned now. What he chose to do was his business, but Cymbril could leave the Rake with a clear conscience.

"Stay away from those old women and their markets," Wiltwain said quietly, and left Cymbril to her lunch.

You're welcome, she thought as he strode away.

At the tent's door flap, something landed squarely at Wiltwain's feet, nearly tripping him: a green-black, bumpy something like a wet rock—the fat frog. It sat there puffing its throat until he edged past it with a scowl. Then the frog stared at Cymbril until a baker's boy shooed it away with a broom handle.

The frog had likely heard her. It would tell its mistresses what Cymbril had said about them. She needed to get off this Rake—and quickly.

As she ate, she thought about the Night Market and Rombol's knowledge of it. He'd insisted that no such things took place. But that was a lie—Cymbril should have guessed he was aware. Why else would Byrni have been in the skeletons' booth? Rombol had sold Byrni to the skeletons, or to the Eye Women, or to *someone* on that magical forest deck. Now she knew why the storerooms in her hidden hallway were mostly empty. The Master had found buyers for the magician's charts, bottles, trunks, and maps—and they weren't the buyers who strolled through daytime markets.

Of *course* Rombol knew. She hoped he also knew now that the Eye Women weren't his most loyal of tenants . . . and where he stood with Brigit.

The afternoon wasn't easy. The crowds liked Cymbril fine as a soloist, but after the fun of the morning, she couldn't get her heart back into singing. The world seemed both wondrous and unbearably sad, both cramped and vast. Night was coming. It was as if the air were getting heavier, harder to move through. "Have courage," Urrt had said. Hand firmly gripping the treasures in her pocket, Cymbril watched the fireflies floating as silent sparks all across the garden plots and in the woods beyond the ditch.

She had just finished "The Evening Bell," and the thinning crowd was asking for more, when Rombol stood in the market's center and called, "Roll it up!" Down came the awnings. Up rolled the mats. Coin boxes snapped shut and jingled onto high wagon seats. Tents whispered into fallen piles of night. Cymbril stood still in the wagon bed, gazing at the first stars. Tomorrow evening, if all went well, she would be seeing them from the Fey realm.

As the twilight deepened, she took a crank basket to the highest deck and stood at the rail, watching darkness fill the hollows and ravines of the wide country. Crickets shrilled and

Rake birds came home to roost. Smoke drifted in blue-gray columns from cottage cook fires. Thinking of the families that lived in the villages, she felt an ache in her chest. Out there, fathers pulled off muddy boots, hung hats on pegs; mothers ladled soup, rocking the young in their arms, humming softly as the world went to sleep. She thought of children laughing, running in and out across the thresholds of homes that did not roll, but stayed in one place, fixed to the earth beneath the stars. Cymbril remained at the rail until full dark. The wind that lifted her hair was full of the scent of hay and warmth, horses and tilled soil.

Though she wasn't hungry for the mushroom soup served in the maidservants' galley, she forced herself to eat well. She would need strength before her next meal. Then, dressed in her faded gray skirt and her oldest white blouse, she went down to see Urrt a final time. This evening she had no tears left.

Urrt smiled when he saw her, as if the world were not such an uncertain place. She sank onto the floorboards beside his feet, and for a long time neither Cymbril nor Urrt spoke. She was thinking of the countless talks they'd had in the rumbling, humid dark. She'd always felt safe there. The Urrmsh were as permanent as mountains. It seemed to her that the Strongarms had somehow transcended grief and pain. They moved the heaviest loads, and yet they were the happiest of creatures. She'd never imagined the evening would come when she could no longer creep down to the Pushpull Chamber and find peace.

"Urrt," she said at last, raising her head.

"Yes, nightingale?"

"Will I see you again?"

"Almost certainly. Has that been troubling you?"

She hadn't expected such a simple, pleasant answer. "I will?"

He blinked placidly. "I won't be spending all my life on the Rake, either. Too much to do in the wide world. I have relatives in the Fey country. I've visited them before. I'll visit them again. It won't be hard finding you, little thrush. I'll just go where the crowds are thickest."

Cymbril smiled. Urrt was the only one who could always make her smile. Among the Urrmsh, it was easy to believe all the wide roads of life converged in one place, and that it was a happy one. She gazed up at him fondly. As her chin began to tremble, she sprang to her feet. If she didn't leave the Pushpull Chamber now, it would become impossible. She touched his hand and leaned her head against one enormous arm. "Promise me once more, Urrt, that we'll talk again. It's the only way I can walk out of here."

"Then, I promise, Cymbril."

She looked from his face to those of all the Armfolk she could see, and she backed slowly away. "Thank you all," she said, not wanting to raise her voice. They waved their hands, smiled with unquenchable affection, and kept pushing, pulling, and singing.

"The song is about you," said one of the Urrmsh beside her as she reached the door. "It has only a beginning so far."

Cymbril bowed and ran for the stairs.

Cymbril lay in her bunk, the treasures glowing beside her. Blinking in their magical half-light, she tried to rest. Mostly she stared at the ceiling, and the Rake rolled on. Several times she got up and checked her door. She was not locked in. But she also kept the door firmly shut against the dark corridor outside.

When she felt the Rake slow at last and begin a turn, she brushed her hair. Leaving everything but the treasures, Loric's wire, and the clothes she wore, she slipped out of her room.

She pulled the door shut as quietly as possible and was just turning to hurry down the corridor when a small pale shape flitted out of the gloom toward her.

Miwa! Cymbril knelt, extending her hands, supposing her old friend had come to say goodbye. But when the cat drew near, Cymbril saw that she held something carefully in her mouth—a cluster of leaves, carried by the stems. Miwa put her forepaws on Cymbril's knee and dropped the leaves into her lap, then peered meaningfully at her.

Cymbril petted Miwa and, wondering, picked up one of the dark green leaves. It was vaguely the shape of an oak leaf and had the scent of mint. Germander. Cymbril was certain it was germander, plucked from a garden on the top deck. One of her favorite songs mentioned "lily, germander, sweetbrier, and columbine," and she'd been curious enough to find each of them, with a gardener's help, to see what they looked like. But why had Miwa brought her five leaves of germander?

"Have you been speaking with Loric?" Cymbril whispered. "Did he tell you to bring these?"

The cat blinked in her languid way and rubbed her silvery face against Cymbril's hand. Miwa waited until Cymbril had put the leaves in her pocket. Then, without ceremony, the cat scampered away and vanished around the corner, too quick for Cymbril to follow.

Cymbril shrugged inwardly, guessing her questions would be answered soon.

The sky was still dark. Mosses and ferns were soaked with dew, but the moon had set. No one stirred in the quiet alleys and halls through which Cymbril glided, wrapped in her claw-shredded cloak, to Rombol's quarters. She stayed alert for any piglike grunting, any hint of movement.

Outside the Master's ironbound door, the corridor's ceiling was open, folded back to let in the summer air. The opposite wall wore a prodigious curtain of vines, like a leafy cliff. Hidden among the foliage a few paces away was an alcove with no floor, in which a ladder was fixed to the wall. Cymbril parted the leaves and stood on the ladder's flat rungs. She turned to face the corridor. From here she could peep out through the vines, but no one in the hallway would see her. She had only to listen so that no one would surprise her by coming up the ladder from the storage spaces below. She kept her breathing silent. Her pulse raced.

The Rake bumped to a stop. At the edge of her hearing, footsteps drummed on the bow. Rombol would be able to feel and hear these things, too. If he was anxious to start the day, he might already be up, splashing water on his face (did Rombol wash his face?). There would not be a moment to waste.

After what seemed ages, someone approached from the left—one set of footfalls and the clanking of armor. Then a man-at-arms crossed in front of Cymbril, and she ducked backwards.

He stopped at Rombol's door. Clothing rustled. Now Cymbril was watching again as the guard rose from his crouch and passed her hiding place with a yawn.

She could barely wait until he had shuffled away toward the barracks. When the hall was quiet, Cymbril looked around and stepped forward. Biting her lip, she hurried to Rombol's door. As she knelt and drew the wire from her sleeve, a sound came from behind the door's timbers—the creak of mattress ropes? Cymbril tensed, ready to sprint away. There was a long silence and then muffled snoring. *Good.*

Lowering herself to her stomach, she felt as if her heart were thrashing at the back of her throat. The crack under the door was darker than the dim hall. She couldn't see the key that the guard had pushed through—but it must be there. Gently, she inserted the wire under the door's right corner and slid it slowly, slowly, to the left. At about the middle, it tapped against something. The key!

Eagerly, Cymbril pulled the wire out and bent the end into a large hook. Then she put it under the door again, pulling it from behind the key in a slow, scooping motion.

On the fourth try, the key emerged. It was heavy and ornate, like the key to some lost chest of ancient jewels. She forced herself to keep her movements calm as she plucked it from the floor and rose to her knees.

Directly behind her, something growled.

Cymbril jerked, almost dropping the key and the wire.

Broad head level with hers, Bale—the Master's hound—bared his fangs and snarled.

Chapter 18

Barrel Corner

"Good morning, Cymbril," said a voice. A shadowy figure towered over the dog.

Wiltwain.

"I'll take the key, thank you." He stooped and snatched it. Above his sharp nose, his eyebrows furrowed. "A wire hook—very clever. You're using burglar tools. Have you run out of enchantments?"

Bale stopped growling and sat licking his jaws, his hot, foul breath puffing into Cymbril's face. Even on her feet, she was not much taller than the hound.

She'd failed Loric. She was sure Wiltwain would pound on Rombol's door, and her life as she knew it would be over. Instead, the Overseer slid the key back under the door, clamped a hand on the scruff of her neck, and marched her down the corridor. Bale padded beside them until his snuffling nose picked up an interesting scent in Barrel Corner, and he prowled away.

When Cymbril could breathe again, she saw that Wiltwain was steering her back toward her own chamber.

"If there's one quality an Overseer needs, it's knowing how his people think. I've heard the rumors about the woods here, how they lead to the Fey country." He peered sternly down at her, then examined the wire, her burglar tool. For the briefest moment, he almost looked impressed. "We both know that if I brought this matter to Master Rombol, you would not see the light of the sun for a very long time. You might even get to try out the stocks in front of the judgment seat. But I'm of the opinion that one good turn deserves another. It's the first rule of good marketing."

"I thought that was 'Everything has a price,'" Cymbril said in a small voice.

"It's the difference," he said, "between making customers and keeping them. None of us lives alone, Cymbril. We rely on one another."

She did her best not to stare at him, but she wondered at his words.

"You showed loyalty yesterday by warning me of danger. That's a quality to be rewarded above all. It's loyalty that keeps this Rake rolling."

It's the Strongarms, Cymbril thought.

"Here are the terms I offer." Wiltwain stopped and took a firm hold of her shoulders. "I'll forget your act of thievery this once, if you'll forget about Loric. You'll stay away from him altogether. No more bringing him food, no more spying on him when he guides the Rake. Speak to him, and it's the stocks for you. I don't even want to catch you looking in his direction. My task is to see that nothing interferes with his work or yours. If Loric goes missing, I will know precisely who is to blame. And blamed she will be, as the sickle moon is my witness. Is anything I've said unclear or unacceptable?"

Cymbril shook her head, unable to believe she was not being sent back to the kitchens and Mistress Reech, at the very least.

"Good. Now go to your bunk. It's not long till the wake-up call. And, Cymbril—do not ever try to steal from the Master again. The Fey boy belongs to him, and so do you."

With a bow, Cymbril dashed off before Wiltwain could change his mind.

After the hallway's first bend, she stopped. Leaning against the wall, she covered her face and breathed deeply, her hands shaking. Wiltwain understood things too well. He didn't need to lock her up. The key was back in Rombol's room, and she was out of time. But Loric was waiting. She would have to tell him what had happened. Listening for any noises, she changed directions.

At every step, her frustration grew, replacing the horror of having been caught. Never to speak to Loric again, never to look at him, because he and she were the Master's property. Freedom waited just outside in the summer darkness, and it would not come again. For the rest of her life, she would stand on chests and in wagon beds, the Thrush of the Great Rolling Cage, and even the dresses she wore would be chosen for her. The future weighed so heavily on her that she could hardly breathe.

Slipping around the last corner to Loric's barred door, she put the Star Shard to her forehead. *Loric! Loric, I'm sorry.*

What's wrong, Cymbril?

Wiltwain caught me. He took the key. Loric, I'm so sorry.

Cymbril heard a flurrying thought that made her eyes widen. Then Loric said, *Don't worry. We'll . . . we'll think of another way. Are you all right? Did he punish you?*

He let me go. Cymbril looked around cautiously, keeping her ears open. *But what was that first thing in your mind just now?*

Nothing. All that matters is that you're safe. There will be other days. I'll keep thinking.

No. She was more certain now of what she'd heard. *No, you were thinking. There is a way to free you without the key.*

For a long time, Loric's thoughts were silent. Perhaps he had a way of keeping them to himself.

Loric. Tell me.

The cost is too great. Go back, please, before someone comes. Or someTHING. The nargus is hunting tonight, but I can't tell where.

Cymbril's back tingled, and she turned around, suddenly afraid. The halls were almost completely dark at this hour, some of the lamps having gone out. The narrow moon was down, and the sun still a ways off. She thought of the Eye Women, and the fact that they probably knew that she'd told Wiltwain of their treachery.

Suddenly she remembered Miwa. *I've got the germander from Miwa. What's it for?*

I need it for an enchantment that will help us once I'm free. There's something Miwa told me. But I can't do it with iron around my neck.

But you used my hairpin before. Cymbril was remembering the tricks Loric had done with the biscuits and the cream.

That was the pin's magic. It wasn't coming through me.

She strained to hear the stir in his mind behind the words he formed. *Loric, this is our last chance,* she persisted. *They know I'm trying to free you. Wiltwain says I'm to stay away from you. They'll start locking me in or keeping me on a chain, too. Right now the hatch is open.* She took the stone away from her brow and unbolted his door.

The portal swung open. Kneeling beside Loric, she whispered aloud, "Tell me."

In the faint light of the stone and the hall's single night lamp, his large eyes were clouded. Sadly, he shook his head.

She grabbed his wrists. "Your home is just down the hill. Do you want to go there or not?"

"I want to go there more than anything. With you."

The racing of her heart was not entirely from fear or urgency. Quite close up, she looked into his gold-brown eyes. Tears were pooling there. "Whenever I try to bring you a key, I fail. So tell me this other way."

Drawing a slow breath, he gently took her hand.

She looked down but made no move to pull her hand away.

"You saved my life in the swamp," he said.

"Loric? Why won't you tell me how to free you?"

For a long time, he watched her. Then, tenderly, his long fingers touched her face.

"It's a magic lock," he said at last. "A sorcerer must have made it for Rombol, or a witch. It can't be smashed with any hammer or cut with any pincers. It opens only for a key, or . . ."

"Or what?"

"Or we stick your magic hairpin into the keyhole and release the power it contains. It will blow the lock apart like a thunderbolt through a daisy. But it will destroy the hairpin, too."

Cymbril froze with her mouth open. It was as if she'd leaned against some great soundless bell that had just rung. She felt its deep vibrations rolling through her bones. All she could hear was her own breath, rushing in and out.

"You see?" said Loric. "That's unthinkable. It would be a mistake to part with that." He pressed her hand. "Now, go out and close my door. Even if it means wearing this collar, I'd rather be here than somewhere you're not."

Cymbril stood up, her knees wobbly, and backed away. Reaching into her pocket, she felt among the leaves and grasped the pin—her mother's gift, the hairpin that no one could take from her.

"Go," said Loric, nodding.

She looked out past the threshold. There was no one in the hallway, no one coming, not a murmur in the still hour before dawn.

With a suddenness that made Loric flinch, she flew to his side and thrust the pin into the lock. "Call the power," she said quietly, not daring a last look down at the perfect gem. Instead, she stared into Loric's eyes. Cymbril had her mother's voice and face, her mother's blood in her veins. She could live without the pin if losing it meant setting him free. "Loric. Do it now."

Eyes brimming, he uttered a swift phrase in the language of the Sidhe.

The hairpin's stone blazed brighter than ever before. Its shank glowed red as if heated in a fire. Cymbril turned away from the glare. Then came a clap of thunder.

When she opened her eyes, the padlock lay in red-hot chunks. The hairpin was gone. All that remained of its stone was a sprinkling of tiny grains, as of crushed crystal, their light fading to darkness. Heavy smoke filled the room, and Loric lay on his side. As Cymbril pulled open the iron collar, he sat up.

"Cymbril," he whispered. Even with his resistance to iron, the collar had left brown-purple bruises around his neck.

"Quickly." She drew him to his feet and led the way.

The noise of the explosion would bring people running. To slow the pursuit for an extra moment, she closed the door and rebarred it. Then, with Loric at her heels, she pelted to the nearest crank basket, dragged him inside it, and cranked for all she was worth. Too slowly, the levels crept past as they descended.

"What about the enchantment?" she asked breathlessly over the squeaking crank. "Shall I give you the germander?"

"Not yet," he said. "We have to wait for Miwa."

With luck, the soldiers would expect her and Loric to go over the rail and down a rope. Already, she heard shouts above. Somewhere Bale began to bark. The fierce, deep sound rang in the bulkheads, seeming to come from all sides at once.

One level up from the bottom, the basket creaked into an archway that gave them a view across the vaulted second story of Barrel Corner, its floor one deck below. The balcony they were passing faced another, beyond the gulf of empty air. This farther colonnaded platform held barrels and plank boxes in stacked rows. Lamps on wall hooks flickered at intervals.

Loric seized Cymbril's arm. "Look," he whispered.

On the far balcony, one by one, the lamps were going out. It was as if a wind extinguished them, but there was no wind. They went dark in order from farther ones to nearer, marking the progress of some unseen force that consumed the light.

"Don't stop here!" whispered Loric.

Cymbril stood rooted, unable to look away from the opposite side of Barrel Corner. She felt him fighting her for the crank.

Something alive—something very *large*—moved behind the barrels, through the narrow aisles, keeping pace with the advancing darkness. As it passed, the stacks rippled askew, some boxes tumbling out of place. Above the sounds of sliding crates and wobbling barrels came a low-pitched grunting, a wet snuffling of the kind made by a hound following a scent, only louder by far—and the *thump, thump* of massive feet. Two barrels fell from the stack and into the avenue, where they crashed on the floor.

"Go! Go!" hissed Loric. They worked the crank together.

Just as the last lamp wavered out, the noises stopped. A sudden stillness flooded the two-story passage. Painfully conscious of the crank's loud screeching, Cymbril and Loric held still. The basket swung and squeaked, its upper rim even with the balcony floor. Crouching, they peeked over the deck. Fear tightened Cymbril's throat. She could scarcely breathe.

Far away, Bale still barked. The only light was filtered up from below, where lamps burned along the first floor of the avenue. Red glimmers and shadows shifted on the carved angels and gargoyles, making their faces seem to contort in terror.

Cymbril risked a glance at Loric.

"Is it gone?" she mouthed.

He shook his head uncertainly.

Reaching an unspoken agreement, they took hold of the crank again, and after a long pause, they began to turn it.

On the other balcony, the closest rank of barrels and boxes splintered as if struck by a wagon at full speed. Kegs of ale and wine flipped end over end. Cymbril and Loric screamed together as an enormous shape pounced across the gulf, straight toward them.

Chapter 19

The Black Nargus

The nightmarish creature landed on the balcony's edge, smashing the rail. Its forelegs ended in curving claws, and its slick-looking fur was like that of a mole. The head was almost entirely a nose—the tiniest black eye-beads above huge, gaping nostrils. Beneath the nose, spittle dripped from a mouth of hooklike teeth.

The nostrils widened and quivered, and the beast bellowed, its pitch so low that Cymbril's bones tingled. The nargus sank its claws into the planks of the balcony, its enormous body sliding backwards. Its leap had not carried it fully across the void, and the monster was struggling to pull itself up, its hindquarters dangling in space. The claws dug furrows in the wood.

"Run!" said Loric into Cymbril's ear.

They leaped out of the basket and dashed along the balcony, dodging between barrels and cloth sacks. Behind them, the beast roared in fury. Just ahead, where another avenue joined Barrel Corner, the balcony ended. The doorways into the bulkhead were blocked by a row of crates. Cymbril saw no escape. Beyond the rail, the passage floor was too far below. Though she didn't dare look backwards, she could hear the nargus loping, its heavy feet pounding. Already it was only a few strides behind them. It grunted, then shook the air with another roar.

Loric caught Cymbril's hand. "Faster!" he yelled. "Come on!"

She ran with him, seeing nothing but the balcony rail, closer and closer—and past it, only empty air. No—not empty. At the last instant, she guessed Loric's plan, and it was totally mad. Out in the middle of the side corridor hung one of the Rake's long-forgotten chandeliers, a giant structure of wooden rings, tarnished candle holders, and glass bangles. Loric shouted, "JUMP!"

Together they stepped up onto the rail and launched themselves. They grabbed hold of the chandelier in a chaos of glass and dust. Overhead, the supporting chain groaned as they swung.

"Let go!" Loric cried. Cymbril closed her eyes as they plummeted down onto a pile of bulging sacks. Grain bags. Sliding to the floor among toppling cargo, she saw that they'd come down safely on the farther section of Barrel Corner's second level—they'd ridden the chandelier across the side passage.

They looked back just in time to watch the nargus crash headfirst into the returning chandelier. Wooden hoops snapped apart. Glass beads rattled like hail. Claws slashing, the monster fell with the ruined chandelier to the corridor floor, one level down. The deck cracked beneath its weight.

Shaking itself free of the wreckage, the creature raised its head and unleashed a terrible roar like prolonged thunder. The nearest wall lanterns went out in an expanding circle of darkness. Even so, in the street's firelight, Cymbril could see the nargus's whole body for the first time. Part bear, part mole, it was larger than a war horse, with corded muscles and a short hairless pink tail.

On the main street level, soldiers approached. At the moment, that hardly seemed a bad thing.

"Miwa," Loric said quietly, moving away from the rail. He turned toward the balcony's length ahead. His gaze seemed far away as he focused his mind's eye, searching with his Sidhe sense for the cat.

Cymbril didn't know what plans had passed between Miwa and Loric, but she wanted to run while the nargus couldn't see them. *But it can smell the Star Shard,* she reminded herself. *No matter where we go, it will come after us.*

Small places. She and Loric had to get out of the open, into a space where the nargus couldn't follow.

The deck was piled with grain sacks and rows of barrels. Loric urged Cymbril forward. But on the main level of Barrel Corner, straight beneath their feet, the monster snuffled and growled, keeping pace with them.

"The Eye Women have sent it after us," Loric muttered. "They don't want us to escape alive."

Cymbril shot him a glance as they ran. "Why?" Were the crones getting revenge for what she'd told Wiltwain?

A moving lantern flared ahead. Voices echoed, and running feet hammered the flooring. Loric and Cymbril skidded to a halt. They were cut off. More soldiers charged straight toward them.

Cymbril glanced desperately around for somewhere to hide. The only chance was to crouch quietly among the rows of cargo and hope the soldiers came along a different aisle. Too late, she realized that she no longer heard the snuffling on the lower floor.

The nargus lunged over the rail to their right. It plowed

through a wall of sacks, its mouth agape. The hideous jaws slammed together just short of her arm, the monster's foul breath on her face as Loric pulled her away. The beast's claws floundered in the loose, sliding bags, finding no traction. Cymbril fell back against Loric, his arms wrapped around her. They stumbled over a sack and pitched to the floor.

So close its vile saliva sprayed them, the nargus waggled its head, its feet scratching for purchase. Again it roared, and Cymbril felt a ringing in her skull.

Men-at-arms raced from between rows of wares. Some hung back in horror. A brave one leaped forward, brandishing his halberd. The monster's teeth smashed shut on the weapon's handle, snapping it. The creature flailed sideways, slamming into the armored man. He flew through the air and struck a mound of boxes.

The nargus regained its footing, its slavering jaws searching for a target. A second man attacked and did no better than the first. The blow of his ax went wide. Gyring its head, the beast flipped the soldier high over the rail.

The man's dagger clattered free of its sheath, landing just beside Loric, who snatched it up.

"No!" cried Cymbril, thinking he meant to lunge at the nargus.

But Loric plunged the blade into a sack, ripping a long

slash in the cloth. Dark, dry beans showered out, rattling and bouncing.

The nargus rushed at him. Loric hurled a double handful of beans straight into the wet caverns of its nostrils. The beast writhed, clawing at its nose, bringing down more barrels. As the men tried to surround it, Cymbril and Loric slinked away, huddling low.

"This way!" Loric turned left around a stack of crates, heading for the wall. He'd left the dagger behind. *Just as well,* Cymbril thought—against the nargus, the dagger would be useless. "Are you all right?" Loric asked, and she nodded. Unlatching an ironbound door, he led her down an enclosed stairway in the dark. Cymbril felt cobwebs sticking to her face and hair, and the air smelled musty and dead. She pulled out the Star Shard and kept close at Loric's heels, trying to keep from falling headlong.

She remembered the wide, low-ceilinged space at the foot of the stairs. It was a storage cellar beneath Barrel Corner, perhaps more often used in years past, but now cluttered with things rarely needed—sawhorses, scaffolds, empty barrels, ladders, old-fashioned lanterns . . . Cymbril had explored it a few years previously and had found nothing of particular interest.

The beam-supported ceiling shuddered with thumps

and roars, with clashes and muffled shouts. On the wooden street just overhead, Rombol's men-at-arms were fighting the nargus.

"That won't go well," said Loric, gazing upward.

Cymbril sat on a rusted stove, catching her breath. "At least we're safe for now. I don't think the nargus can get down here."

"Yes, it can." Loric scooted a broken chair aside, clearing a space on the floor. "Narguses can collapse their skeletons and squeeze into places you wouldn't believe."

Cymbril stared at him. "Then we have to keep moving. We have to get to the aft hold." Now she understood how the monster had stayed hidden. Except for the doors of counting-houses and living quarters, there were no barriers on the Rake. The nargus used the crawlspaces above dropped ceilings, beneath raised floors—untraveled half-levels just like this one. Bale could smell the creature but not easily reach it. And to Rombol's men, it would seem the hound was barking at nothing. Fear squeezed Cymbril's chest, making it hard to breathe. The beast was hunting her and Loric now, just as the cats hunted mice.

No sooner had she thought of cats than Miwa bounded out of the shadows, her eyes shining in the Fey stone's light.

Close behind her, two other cats followed—the counting master's yellow tom and a sleek black cat Cymbril didn't recognize.

She looked wonderingly from the cats to Loric. "What—?" she began.

"The germander," said Loric, holding out a hand.

Cymbril yelped and ducked her head as something heavy crashed to the street above them. The battle sounded horrible, with men yelling, screaming in terror and pain. Footsteps charged to and fro. And always, the ghastly deep roar of the nargus made objects rattle and the floor thrum. Cymbril had the impression that the roaring she could hear was only the several topmost notes of a vast chord, a voice that extended down and down beyond the limit of hearing.

Numbly, she pulled the germander leaves from her pocket and handed them to Loric.

Kneeling quickly, he arranged the five leaves on the floor in an arced line, a fan spreading before him. The three cats watched, and Cymbril wondered what sort of spell he was about to cast. He was free of the iron collar at last. Cymbril had a sudden memory of how Brigit had regarded him with fear. Although Cymbril trusted Loric, a shivery thrill ran through her—what was he capable of now? Loric held his hands out, palms downward, over the leaves. He spoke in the Sidhe language, and at once the germander leaves burst into blue flames.

Cymbril gaped as the five fires leaped from the floor to merge into a single orb that hovered between Loric's hands, so bright that she had to squint. The germander leaves were gone, consumed. Suddenly the fiery ball divided itself, a part of it shooting like a meteor into each cat. Cymbril cried out as blue flames engulfed the cats and they tumbled to the floor, rolling, then rose to chase their tails and dance crazily, balanced on their hind legs like people.

Cymbril seized Loric's arm. "What did you do?"

"They're all right," he said.

One brilliant tongue of fire had remained floating in the air, the last fragment of the orb. Loric seemed puzzled by it. Whizzing, it streaked over the cats and swooped behind a pile of broken furniture. The ceiling above and the surrounding debris flared with its intense radiance.

"What's that?" Cymbril asked.

Before Loric could answer, a deafening roar sounded just behind them.

The head and front claws of the nargus dangled from the stairwell. Clinging together, Cymbril and Loric floundered backwards. Even the light of the Star Shard dimmed in the monster's presence.

Twisting itself like a gimlet, the enormous beast oozed through the narrow opening. Plopping into the sublevel, it puffed its bones back into place and became again a mountain of fury. The soldiers above must have attacked it with fire. Red welts scarred the huge head and side where the fur had burned away. Its eyes fixed on Cymbril, who clutched the blue-green stone. The nargus roared, its mouth stretching impossibly wide, the hooked teeth swiveling forward. A blast of fetid breath blew Cymbril's hair back, and she screamed.

Loric pushed her behind him, putting himself between her and the horror. For one instant, his eyes met hers, and she saw that he was ready to die for her—ready to meet the monster head-on, so that she might have a chance to flee.

A silvery blur flashed past them.

A lithe, slender figure vaulted at the nargus—a form like that of a person, yet covered in fur. Cymbril glimpsed an outstretched arm, a hand with the pale fingers spread. Sharp claws emerged suddenly from the fingertips and raked the nargus across the snout.

The figure landed on the monster's back, delivered three

more vicious claw swipes, and was somersaulting away before the nargus had finished its bellow of outrage.

Two more agile shapes struck at the nargus, one from the left, one from the right.

The first of the three alighted at a crouch before Cymbril, and she found herself eye to eye with a person both human and feline. The arms, legs, and much of the face were distinctly humanoid. But the entire body glistened with short silver fur. Large cat ears crowned the head, and the mouth was catlike, the upper lip divided and whiskered.

"Miwa?" Cymbril could hardly believe what she saw. She recognized her old friend by the color of her fur and by her eyes.

"Go!" said Miwa in a woman's voice. "The far stairway. We'll catch up with you."

Behind Miwa, the yellow tom and the black cat were also half-human. They taunted the nightmare beast, staying just out of its reach.

"It will lose interest in us," Miwa hissed. "Go quickly!" Then she spun back to the fight, springing through the air.

Stairway. Yes. Cymbril forced herself to think. There was a second stairway, on the other side of Barrel Corner. She led Loric to it and clambered up ahead of him, glancing again at the battle. "What are they?" she asked.

"Ferials," he said, close behind her. "Upwalkers. Those Who Go on Two Legs."

"People who turn into cats?" Cymbril winced as the nargus cuffed the tom, who slid over the floor, smashing through a heap of metal scraps.

"No." Loric pushed her upward. "Animals who can take a form close to human. These three are felid ferials— upwalkers of the cats."

Cymbril stuck her head through the stairwell's hatch and looked across the wide avenue. Near the other stairway, the soldiers were tending to their wounded. A haze of smoke hung over the wreckage of a cart and shattered barrels. If she and Loric kept to the shadows, they could probably pass down the street unnoticed.

She warned Loric of the danger, and, moving quickly, they flitted into the murk beneath the loggia. In moments the battle's aftermath was well behind them.

Thinking through the shortest route to the aft hold, Cymbril glanced at Loric as they ran. "Why did Miwa need you to cast that spell?"

"The ferials had only just arrived on the Rake when the Eye Women recognized them for what they were. Those witches placed an enchantment on them that trapped them in their cat forms. They've been unable to change for years. The

Eye Women want to dominate all magic on the Rake. Ferials are too powerful—the Sisters had to control them."

"Couldn't someone at the Night Market have helped them?"

Loric shook his head. "Not there, where the Sisters rule everything."

"Why didn't the ferials just leave the Rake, then? They could have gone to the Sidhe, or—"

"They couldn't leave," Loric began, "because—"

The withering roar of the nargus stopped him in mid-sentence. Cymbril looked back and saw the monster charging down the center of Barrel Corner, following the Star Shard. Her heart sank. Panic beat around her like a cloak in a high wind.

Loric's eyes told her not to give up. His grip on her wrist was firm.

She shook dread from her mind. "This way." She took Loric into a side lane—Bottle Alley—and chose another climbing stair. *Up. Down. Confuse the nargus.* This stairway was an external addition to the passage, only a framework of beams and slat steps. She could feel the monster's black eyes watching her, and she longed to be hidden.

A sudden thought came to her. *I could put the Star Shard*

down. I could leave it behind, and the nargus couldn't smell us anymore. She glanced at the radiant stone in her hand, the gift from her father. A whirl of panic threatened again to overwhelm her.

She faltered at the stairway's top, pressing the stone to her chest. Loric looked at her searchingly.

Below, the monster slammed into the stairway's base, not slowing, its limbs scrabbling to drag its bulk upward. But it was too big for the flimsy structure. Railings flew apart. Nails shrieked, yanked from their holes. Stairs buckled, and still the nargus climbed, plowing, destroying the steps that supported it. Halfway up, the framework gave way completely, and the creature fell back to the floor amid a storm of timbers. Opening its cavernous maw, it let loose its roar. Its hide still smoked from the soldiers' fire, and Cymbril caught the reek of charred flesh. Shrugging the boards aside, the nargus hurled itself against the wall and buried its claws.

"It's coming up!" Loric said.

Again Cymbril ran with him. They ducked through a candle makers' workshop, where early rising chandlers and apprentices stared at them, tracing holy symbols in the air to ward off evil. They'd heard the pandemonium in Barrel Corner.

"It's chasing us!" Cymbril yelled to them. "Go out that way!"

At the workshop's far end, an open window led out onto the balcony of Horseshoe. Cymbril led the way half around it, through the moss garden at its apex, and down a flight to the Doll Makers' Court. She turned left at an intersection she knew well, where the doll makers had hung from a post a jointed, life-size wooden puppet whose costume they changed each season.

Dashing over the dark, rippling canal by the Kind-bridge, its pillars carved into a thousand tiny faces of people and animals, she steered Loric up the quiet lane of Dusk. Workshops and merchants' dwellings alternated with stretches of trellis that walled and roofed the passage, the lattice twined with dark-growing aromatic herbs. Some of Rombol's earliest risers had begun their day's routine, preparing for the market. Others clustered nervously, awakened by the clamor, exchanging rumors that strange and terrible things were afoot in the fading night.

Cymbril and Loric descended past a final view of the canal, a pole lantern paving the water's surface with a pathway of gold. They stood still a moment, trying to get their breath back. Cymbril realized they'd heard no sounds of pursuit since Bottle Alley.

Peering out across the water, they listened to it lapping the hulls of the barges and punts.

Cymbril felt Loric take her hand. His touch was warm and comforting. She gazed into his luminous brown eyes, remembering how he'd stood between her and the nargus. She longed to be out of danger, safe with him somewhere far from the Rake . . .

"Don't stop here," said a voice.

With a start, Cymbril looked around.

Miwa darted from between blue nightberry hedges along the canal, still in her graceful womanlike shape. The jet-black ferial emerged behind her, also female, with a more angular face. The male came third, the yellow tom who had been with Cymbril at the prow on the night when the nargus had made its presence known. Blood oozed from a cut on the tom's shoulder, but he greeted Cymbril with a rakish bow. For the first time, Cymbril noticed that they retained the long, articulated tails of cats—proportionately larger to suit their human stature.

Cymbril pocketed the Star Shard and wonderingly touched Miwa's forearm and hand. The claws were retracted now, and the hand felt soft, its palm like a cat's paw pads.

"Where is the nargus?" asked Loric.

"We wove a spell," said the dark ferial in a lilting accent. "The nargus took a wrong turn, following a false scent. But there's little time. The soldiers are hunting you, too."

Cymbril shook her head, so full of questions that she hardly knew what to say. "For so long," she said to Miwa, "I've wished you could talk to me."

The silver ferial smiled. "It would have made things easier." Pulling Cymbril by the hand, she led the group down the final flight of steps. It was not far now to the aft hold, where Urrt had promised to leave a hatch open.

"You've always helped me," Cymbril said as they walked. "For as long as I can remember."

The ferial nodded. "It was a duty we were given, a magical binding, though I must admit, I've enjoyed it far more than I expected."

"It's cost us nothing," said the male, following at the rear. "We have nine lives, you know, and these years under the spell don't even count as one."

"A duty?" Cymbril asked. "I don't understand."

They had reached the lower hallway now. The daytime lamps hadn't been lighted yet, but a single night torch cast enough shine for Cymbril to make out the door of the hold.

"We were bidden to watch over you," Miwa said. "To

protect you from harm with our lives. More than one of them, if it came to it."

Cymbril blinked. "But who—?"

The ferial held up a hand. "There's no time to give you the full story. Let's just say that there is one concerned with your welfare, who asked us to keep an eye on you for as long as you were aboard this Rake. When you leave, our duty will be fulfilled and the binding undone."

The other female winked at Cymbril. "You never saw me at all, did you? I kept my distance, working the perimeter."

Miwa gazed toward the hold, then took Cymbril by the shoulders. "This is farewell, Cymbril. When you're off the Rake—truly free, and not just at a market—then the spell will take us back to the time and place at which it was cast. More than nine years ago! I don't know if we'll remember this or not."

Cymbril searched her friend's eyes. "If I meet you again, you may not even know me."

The ferial nodded ruefully. "That is possible. But be the same, and I'll like you again."

Cymbril threw her arms around Miwa, burying her face in the woman-cat's soft warmth. "Thank you, Miwa."

Miwa started to reply, but the words caught in her throat, and she only held Cymbril tightly and stroked her hair. When she found her voice again, the ferial said, "By the way, my name is Memenisse—Miwa was your idea. Memenisse. Remember it. You may need to know it someday."

Still in Memenisse's embrace, Cymbril gave her hands to the other ferials, thanking them.

"Be well and happy, Cymbril," said the tom.

Cymbril touched Memenisse's face, where the downy fur was wet with tears. "You can cry," she whispered.

"Only when we're half-human. Now, go."

Cymbril pulled away, lifting her hand in a wave.

But there came a rustle of movement. At the far end of the passage, just beyond the hold's door, a man stepped around the corner.

Cymbril heard Memenisse growl.

The man had a strange, unkempt appearance. He was not one of Rombol's people. Short and broad, he had a giant belly and stood on wide, bare feet.

"You!" Memenisse spat the word. "Stay back! Let them pass."

Cymbril glanced at Loric, who stared at the man, slightly frowning.

The stranger was dressed like a beggar, one piece of cloth tied around his waist as a crude skirt, another doubled over him, his head through a hole ripped in the center.

"You thick-skulled longtail," said the man, approaching on bandy legs. His eyes were wide-set and round, with droopy bags beneath them. He had fat lips and thinning hair that clung wetly. "'Let them pass,' you say? Yarn-batting nitwit! You think this girl would be alive with no other protection than yours?"

The black ferial and the tom flanked Loric and Cymbril, crouching with hands raised menacingly at the stranger, claws out. All three were growling, the fur on their backs standing up.

"Loric," Cymbril whispered, "who is he?"

"Master Ranunculus," said Loric.

Memenisse muttered, "The fat frog."

Cymbril stared at the odd, waddling man. The sorcerer—"R," the owner of the magic books and everything else in the secret storerooms. He hadn't vanished in the swamp, after all.

"*They* did it!" Cymbril blurted, understanding. "The Eye Women turned you into the frog." She remembered how Loric's orb of fire had divided, the final part shooting away behind the stacked furniture. It had restored another who was trapped in a form imposed by the Sisters' magic—the fat frog, who had been hiding there.

Ranunculus scowled in disgust. "They were always jealous of me. They've gotten most of my possessions from Rom-bol, thanks to you." He eyed Cymbril darkly.

"I'm sorry," she said, but couldn't manage to feel too guilty, remembering the unwholesome nature of the books and the way that the frog had always watched her. "You followed me everywhere."

"Protecting you," said Ranunculus. "Blocking my cousins' spells. Time and again they tried to turn you into something far nastier than me."

"Why would they do that? I'm not powerful."

The sorcerer's lip curled. "More so than you think. The witches never liked you. But what made them *hate* you was that you robbed them. A dozen years of their work snatched away."

"What are you talking about?" Cymbril asked.

Somewhere overhead, the nargus roared.

"There's no time for this," said Memenisse. "It's coming."

Ranunculus brushed past them all, the ferials baring their teeth, backs arched and bristling. The sorcerer stretched his joints as he walked. He popped his neck and cracked his knuckles. Flexing his fingers, he drew sparks from the tips, and Cymbril knew he was preparing for battle. He faced the direction of the nargus's approach.

Once more, he glanced over his shoulder at Cymbril. "Those young twins, the Curdlebrees. My cousins were stealing their minds and spirits, year by year—it's a slow process. I tried to slow it further, but another few months, and they would have been empty vessels. The witches would have abandoned their withered old bodies and taken over the new ones. Young again! They must have been delighted to sell you that Nixielixir, if they guessed who it was for. But then—" He snorted with laughter. "Yes, you've made enemies of my cousins, girl."

"Hmf! A second life to live," grumbled Memenisse. "Humans striving to be cats."

"Will Gerta and Berta be all right?" Cymbril called after the magician. One level up, the nargus rampaged, much closer. Globes of red flame roared into life in the sorcerer's hands, coalescing from the air.

"You saved those girls," Ranunculus said, his makeshift robes whipping in a rush of wind. "Away from my cousins, their minds and spirits will grow back strong. Now go to your freedom, mischievous imp. Since the elf boy did me a good turn, I'll deal with this black nargus."

From the doorway to the hold, Cymbril called her thanks.

"Oh, I'm no friend of yours," Ranunculus shouted back. "Believe me when I say you wouldn't like me. I protected you to spite my cousins. Now, go!"

He was a dark silhouette against the fires he held, huge spheres of twisting smoke and flame, shot through with inner lightning bolts. Waving to Cymbril and Loric, the ferials retreated past the door, heading for the shadows. On the stairs beyond Ranunculus, the nargus appeared in a vile temper.

Loric tugged Cymbril into the hold and heaved the door shut.

Chapter 20

The Rising of the Sun

The wide, lofty chamber was packed with spice bales, cloth bolts, grain sacks, and boxes stacked in pillars. Cymbril held up the Star Shard for light.

An explosion shook the Rake as Ranunculus unleashed his fires in the corridor outside. A tremor shot through the floor, toppling boxes. Loric and Cymbril fell to their knees and covered their heads. A cabinet dropped from the wall with a crash, and a howling gale swept the hallway. Power crackled and blasted, drowning the roars of the nargus.

Slowly the vibrations ceased, and silence returned. The door behind Cymbril and Loric remained closed.

They threaded forward, stepping over rope coils and spooled carpets. Somewhere in the shadows must be a hatch.

Somewhere . . . but the hold was jammed with tools and merchandise.

Thinking again of Ranunculus, Cymbril glanced at Loric. "Did you mean to turn him back into a human?"

"No. I had no idea he was hiding there, or that the frog was more than a frog."

"And did you notice the cloth he found to wear?" she asked. "Both pieces were of Moonpine blue. Probably Gerta and Berta dyed them."

"Everything in the world is interconnected," Loric said. He closed his eyes and held up both palms. "There!" He pointed toward the far wall.

"Was that a finding spell?" asked Cymbril.

"No," he said. "I feel a draft."

They hurried around a wagon with no wheels, past a barrier of crates, and there it was in the wall: a hatch of timbers banded with iron, so large that Cymbril doubted even a strong man could open it alone. But Urrt had been here. It stood open, hooked in place, just as he had promised. Beside it lay a hefty coil of rope, one end tied to the mooring ring. Dear Urrt!

The night breeze wafted in, bringing the smell of wet grass and plowed earth. A slope fell away from the Rake's side to a dense forest, the trees like black, billowing clouds in the darkness.

"The Greenmouth," Loric whispered. His eyes were wide, gathering the faint light of the stars.

They sat on the threshold, feet dangling. Even from this lowest sublevel above the axles, it was five fathoms to the ground. "Be careful," they both said at once, and smiled.

"You first," said Loric, pitching the rope overboard. "I'm right behind."

"Goodbye, Thunder Rake." Cymbril held the rope in both hands, scissored it between her feet, and made the dizzying, skin-burning slide to the grass. She rolled aside as Loric touched down next to her. They were both drenched at once with dew.

No sooner had Cymbril picked herself up than men shouted overhead. Figures moved between the torches at the rail, pointing. She and Loric had been seen.

Now Loric led, racing down the long bank. Cymbril heard something heavy fall into the grass and glanced back. The men were dropping more coils of rope, the ends fixed to cleats on the lowest deck.

Underfoot, the weeds concealed holes and soft places. Stumbling at nearly every step, she and Loric pulled each other onward, downward, and slowly the line of trees drew nearer.

"Hurry!" Loric gasped. A thistle had lashed his face, leaving a streak of blood. Cockleburs clung to their clothes.

The hound's deep baying rang through the dark. Bale was on the ground now, somewhere behind them to the left. The men yelled. Torch light reflected on the old twisted trunks ahead.

Beneath the first limbs, the grassy slope gave way to a floor of moss. Dodging over crisscrossed roots, Loric swerved into a thicket. "Through here," he said, holding a branch out of Cymbril's way.

She heard soldiers trampling the brush, but the sounds echoed, and she could not tell where the men were. The trees squatted thicker and thicker, lumpy as half-melted candles. Night birds called, their songs haunting and strange. Likely these were birds of the Fey world, perched in the forest's eaves. Bale had stopped barking, but the pursuers were close, their voices floating from all around. Firelight flickered on the forks and arches above. Creepers of moss stirred in the wood's breath.

When Cymbril thought she could go no farther, Loric led her down a bank to the edge of a stream. She gulped air, shivering in her soaked clothes. The steep-sided ravine was almost a tunnel, the trees curving over it, root knuckles clutching its banks.

Loric's eyes gleamed. Even his hair seemed to shine brighter through the burrs that tangled it.

There was nowhere to walk but straight up the streambed, into the current. The water sloshed around their knees, swift and piercing cold. They rounded a final bend, and before them loomed the gate of the Sidhe world. It could be nothing else. The forest ended in a wall of briar and trees, all intertwined so tightly that Cymbril saw no gap for even a squirrel to scurry through. This hedge rose up into the canopy of limbs and leaves. It marched away into darkness on both sides. The stream rushed from an arched tunnel at the wall's base, just large enough for Loric and Cymbril to enter side by side.

Splashing toward it, Cymbril wanted to cry out with relief. They'd made it! A wonderful aroma washed out from the tunnel—something like lilacs, something like new-mown hay under a summer sun, yet not quite like either of them.

"Only those with Sidhe blood can go in," Loric said, squeezing her arm. "Or those the gate watchers allow. Anyone else will not see the tunnel or even the hedge, but only the old forest trooping on and on."

At the mouth of the tunnel, they exchanged a glance and laughed.

Suddenly Loric's eyes widened in horror.

Something hit Cymbril from behind, knocking her face-down into the icy water. The stream penetrated her clothing all at once. Her shriek came out in bubbles. Water flooded into her nose and mouth, bringing the sensation of liquid fire. She groped for handholds in sand and slime as the current pushed her backwards. At last her feet bumped against solid rock, and she struggled upright, coughing out water. Flinging soaked hair from her face, she searched for Loric—and stopped still in dismay.

Bale had found them. The hound stood astride Loric, pinning him in the stream. Bale's jaws gripped Loric's neck, but he did not bite down. Snarling a threat, he held the Sidhe's head out of the water, keeping him a prisoner until Master Rombol arrived. Ears flat, the dog turned his amber eyes toward Cymbril, warning her not to move.

She sagged to her knees, hugging herself. She felt as if the water's ice had frozen her heart. They had been so close—but Rombol had won.

"Cymbril," Loric said quietly. The brook made his hair billow and swirl like the plants beneath the sea at Roadsend.

"This hound isn't going to hurt me. You can make it into Gorhyv Glyn. My parents will take care of you. Someday soon I'll join you there."

Cymbril shook her head. "When we go, we'll go together."

He started to argue, but torches flared through the leaves. The brush thrashed, and soldiers appeared at the top of the bank. The first men hollered to others, reporting that Cymbril and Loric were found.

Wiltwain crashed from the bushes, followed by Rombol himself. Where the roots made a crude staircase, they led their party into the ravine. The men-at-arms were muddy and covered with scratches. Forming a ring around each of the two, the soldiers appeared none too happy to be standing in cold water before sunrise.

Wiltwain glared at Cymbril, hands on his belt, but left words to the Master of the Rake. There was something in the Overseer's gaze more complex than anger. Cymbril realized it was a look of hurt—of disappointment. She had thrown away his mercy and broken her promise to be loyal and good. He kept shaking his head as if he couldn't believe her stupidity.

Rombol trudged to the group surrounding Loric. "Bale!" he said. "Stand down. Good lad."

Bale released Loric and backed away. The hound's muzzle was wrinkled in warning, his tail wagging for Rombol, threshing the water.

Rombol signaled for Cymbril to be brought closer. In her fall, she'd been washed twenty paces downstream. The guards seized her elbows and dragged her forward, dropping her beside Loric.

For an endless moment the Master silently glowered, and it was worse than his most terrible bellowing. In the ravine's chill, his breath emerged as white puffs. He stared into the tree limbs, perhaps to control his rage. Then he looked down at the two and spoke in a dangerous, quiet tone. "The Rake has been your home, Cymbril. This is how you thank me."

Cymbril refused to cower, though she could not control her shivering. She raised her chin and stared back.

"There will be changes now," Rombol said. "And if they are not to your liking, remember who is to blame." He nodded to the guards, who grabbed Loric and Cymbril. The Master turned away.

"Wait!" said Cymbril in the firmest voice she could manage.

Rombol stood still. Wiltwain gave Cymbril a scathing glance and shook his head. *Don't speak,* his expression said.

The Rake's Master slowly faced her. "You have something to say?"

She felt her jaw trembling and willed it to stop. Water from her doused hair trickled into her eyes. "I have a deal to offer you."

Rombol took a slogging step closer. "What?" He wasn't asking what the deal was. It sounded more as if he couldn't believe his ears.

"A deal," she repeated, trying hard to look and sound like Brigit. "All the world is a market. Anything can be had for a price."

Rombol crossed his arms, apparently not flattered to be quoted under these circumstances. He towered above her, waiting.

Cymbril didn't dare to let herself think about what she was doing. Pulling her arm free of the guard's grip, she reached into her pocket.

"Cymbril," said Loric, "no!"

The Star Shard blazed in her hand, its blue-green light dancing on a thousand ripples in the stream.

Most of the guards had never seen the stone before. They gaped or squinted, and one gave a low whistle. Bale growled at it, hackles raised. It lit up the glade as if a star really had fallen to earth.

"Our freedom," Cymbril said, "for this stone."

"More deception," Rombol said. "I know the elf stone will not leave you. It always comes back to the hand of its little mistress."

"It will remain yours if I give it to you." She extended it toward him. "You can make sure of it before we go."

The Star Shard illuminated tears on Loric's cheeks.

"It is a great treasure of my father's people," Cymbril said. "Well worth two slaves who will never serve you happily."

Wiltwain's eyes narrowed as he looked keenly from her to Rombol.

The Master snatched the stone from her. Cymbril gasped as it went. She curled her fingers on emptiness. She would never hold it again, never half glimpse her parents' faces behind its glow.

Gone.

Rombol rubbed it on his shirt, held it up toward one of the torches, and studied it with one eye shut, then the other. "Well," he said at last, shrugging, "it *is* a pretty rock, obviously Sidhe, clearly magical. But not of perfect shape and not all that rare." He looked down sideways at her. "This stone will buy freedom for one of you. Do you have any other deals to make?"

He was thinking of the hairpin, trying to get it as well. "I have nothing else," Cymbril said, still flexing her hand. "I had to give up my hairpin to open Loric's collar. It's gone."

"So is the lock," said Rombol. "And believe me, it did not come cheap. That's destruction of my property. There's been an awful lot of that tonight."

Anger rose within Cymbril. "That one stone is worth much more than you paid for both of us. You know that! If you want it, you must let us go!"

"Must?" Rombol's lip curled, an expression matching Bale's. He looked at the guards, and a few snickered obediently. "You've made your offer," said Rombol. "You've heard mine. Choose now. Does one of you leave the Rake, or do you both come back and learn to be content?"

Cymbril pressed her lips together. The breeze knifed through her wet clothes. She would have to buy Loric's escape. Then she would go back to the Rake, back to punishment—probably chains. And she would no longer have the treasures to comfort her.

"Quickly, girl," said Rombol, "before we all catch our deaths of cold. What will it be?"

She tossed her bedraggled hair. "It will be Loric. Let him go."

"No," said Loric. "I won't go."

Rombol nodded, raising his brows. "Fair and done. Go home, Fey boy. The Rake will manage without you. Swamp travel was not one of my better ideas."

A few guards smiled. None laughed.

Loric started to protest again, but at that moment a bird swooped over his head, twittering. With a curious light in his eye, he fell silent.

"On your guard!" said Wiltwain. "He's up to something."

The soldiers snapped to attention, scanning the woods. Bale sniffed the air.

Cymbril hardly cared what was happening. She'd lost her dearest possessions, and the days ahead seemed as dark as if the sun would never rise. Like a sleepwalker, she got to her feet. Would sunlight feel warm on her face? Would she ever again have the heart to sing?

"There!" Wiltwain pointed to the top of the bank. "Something's coming."

Rombol drew a short sword. The Star Shard's light leaked out through the fingers of his other fist.

The bushes divided. Into the firelight plodded Urrt. Cymbril's heart leaped. She'd never been so happy to see him.

"You are all still here," Urrt said, waddling to the ravine's edge. "Very good, very good."

The night bird sang again from a high limb. Cymbril watched Loric's face. Clearly, he understood what the bird was saying.

Behind Urrt, another of the Rake's Urrmsh trundled out of the forest—and another behind that one.

"What is your business here?" demanded Rombol. His men looked increasingly uncomfortable. Their worst fear, Cymbril thought, must be a rebellion of the Armfolk.

More of the Strongarms appeared, dozens of them, lining the top of the bank. "The kindly bird tells me," said Urrt, "that our Cymbril has just made a purchase from you, Rake Master. Her precious family treasure for the freedom of this Sidhe lad."

"Yes," said Rombol. "And what is that to you, Master Strongarm?"

There were now more than a hundred Urrmsh on the ravine's edge. Cymbril had never seen them move so quickly.

Urrt scratched his warty jaw. "It seems today's marketing has begun early. We are here to do some buying of our own."

At the line's far end, a Strongarm held up a large empty leather sack. From his belt purse, he took a handful of coins— which, when measured by an Urrmsh hand, was a mound of copper and silver. The Strongarm dropped it into the sack and passed it to the next Urrmsh. That one also tossed in money, earned from wages, from feats of strength in the markets—and handed the sack along.

"Nothing is forgotten in the songs of the Urrmsh," said Urrt. "We remember exactly how much you paid for little Cymbril: one hundred pieces of gold. A generous price to offer a starving old woman who would have taken less, but you always strive for fairness, Master Rombol. You knew at first sight that Cymbril was someone extraordinary." He smiled his uneven smile, and the sack came along the line, getting heavier.

An ache rose in Cymbril's throat.

"For Cymbril's freedom," Urrt said, "we offer you the equivalent of one thousand gold pieces—in small denominations, such as we have. Ten times what you paid, for she's developed many qualities since then. It's not nearly as much as she's worth, since our sack isn't big enough. Nor is your vault."

Wiltwain grinned until Rombol looked his way.

"I wasn't really thinking of selling her," the Master grumbled.

"Were you not?" asked Urrt, turning his gaze meaningfully upon the Star Shard.

Rombol might have haggled under the sun in an open market square, Cymbril thought. But a thousand gold pieces was a dazzling sum, and Rombol surely knew he needed the Armfolk much more than they needed him—even he couldn't afford enough horses to pull the Rake. "Fair and done," the Master said.

When Urrt had added his coins, the huge sack bulged, swinging in his grasp. None of the Rake's men would be able to lift it. "I'll carry this for you," said Urrt. "And as a token of your goodwill for the morning's favorable business, perhaps you might send for Loric's clothes. And Cymbril's wardrobe, too, so she can wear her dresses to remember us by."

Cymbril hoped the Urrmsh could see the thankfulness in her eyes. Even if she lived to be older than Mistress Ilda, she'd never be able to repay the Armfolk.

"All agreed," said Rombol, sighing impatiently. "Now, I've had quite enough of the wet and the mud. We have a market to open, and I should like to be dry by then." He turned to Cymbril. The anger was gone from his face. It was not yet daylight, and he'd already made two profitable deals. "I'll have your clothes delivered right there, to that flat boulder on the slope." He looked around into the leafy, gurgling shadows. "So the stories are true. The door to the elf country is in this wood. I suppose you know your way from here?"

"Yes, Former Master," said Loric.

"Well, then," said Rombol. "Goodbye."

Cymbril offered her hand. He grasped it briskly, then strode away, Bale at his heels, the great boots and paws churning the stream. And that was all with him—no sentiment, no backwards glance. Cymbril guessed one must have a hard heart to become as rich as Rombol, but she was glad to be free of the world he ruled.

Wiltwain crouched on one knee, right in the current, and gripped Cymbril's shoulders. "Well bargained."

"Like Brigit?" she asked hopefully.

"Well . . . yes," he said. "But don't strive to be like her. You're much better off as Cymbril." His eyes twinkled, and she saw that he'd forgiven her. She studied his weathered face, strong but deeply lined, his hair beginning to show flecks of gray. She would worry about him, she knew, in the days ahead—about how he would oversee a Rake where witches lurked. Wiltwain had no ferials to help him. At least he had the Armfolk.

"We heard a report just before we found you," he said. "You were right about a wild beast on board. It's apparently dead now, a huge smoldering carcass. Did you see how it was killed?"

"Not exactly," she said truthfully. "We didn't do it."

"Of course not. Well, the Master will be looking into the matter."

"A nargus," Cymbril said, allowing herself a grin that said *I told you so.* "It was called a black nargus."

"You're a walking bestiary," he said.

"Be careful of the two old women. They mean none of us any good." She almost added that Ranunculus was back but thought better of it. She'd already caused the magician enough loss. Let him reveal himself when and if he chose.

"I think we'll meet again, Thrush of the Rake," Wiltwain said. "And I'm certain I'll hear of you."

"I'll come to the markets now and then. When the witches are gone."

He laughed softly and nodded. "Come and sing for us anytime. You name your wage."

A lightness tickled her insides. She could do that. She was free now to do anything . . . to go anywhere her feet would carry her, to stay wherever the stars or the breezes seemed kind.

The guards followed the Master and the Overseer up the steep bank. One by one, the Urrmsh vanished into the forest. With the bag of coins straining over his shoulder, Urrt waved a giant hand.

At last Cymbril and Loric were alone, except for the bird, who seemed overflowing with things to say.

Loric took Cymbril's hands and fell to his knees. Diamonds of water shimmered in his brambly hair. "I haven't thanked you for saving me in the swamp. Now I'll never catch up."

She pulled him to his feet and glanced toward the dark archway into Gorhyv Glyn. "Oh, yes, you will."

They hurried forward. The dim tunnel, scented with sweet, wild growing things, led toward a distant grove of floating mist. Though still piercing, the water no longer made Cymbril shiver.

"I'll find you another Star Shard," said Loric, wading beside her. "I'll never stop looking until I've found just the one."

She slid her hand into his. There were many things she wanted to look for, both in the Fey realm and in the world of humankind. She was born of both. That was another treasure from her parents, one that truly could not be taken or given away.

The tunnel opened into a forest—the trees familiar, yet ancient and tall, leaves rustling in an early breeze. Among the roots spread a carpet of green-gold flowers for as far as Cymbril could see. They shone with their own light, as if the mossy ground were a mirror of the night sky.

The sky! The stars were growing pale, winking out, but she saw more of them than she would have thought possible. No wonder their shards fell to Earth—the heavens hardly had room for so many.

Away beyond the trunks, golden lamplight flickered. Loric and Cymbril climbed onto the stream's bank.

Now from the shadows on every side, dozens of people stepped into view. They were slender, graceful, and fair of face, their clothing of the same shades as the wood and the dusk. Like Loric, they had hair that glistened with the light of stars. They called out in pleasant voices, and Loric answered. Though Cymbril couldn't understand the words, the language seemed as musical as the song of the water.

Cymbril heard her own name several times. The Sidhe smiled at her and offered warm, strong hands to help her onto firmer ground.

"They're keepers of the gate," Loric explained, "guards of our country's edge. The seers of my people have been watching our journey from afar. They knew we were coming."

At the beckoning of a Fey man in a long green coat, his belt glowing like the moon in silver mist, they started along a path that wound to and fro among the trees. In the limbs high overhead nestled houses like giant baskets woven all of branches, blanketed with moss. As Cymbril watched, Sidhe appeared in the windows of some, waving down at her and Loric with pale, lithe hands.

Branches swayed. A man and a woman came along the

path to meet them. Their hair was long, the woman's twined with blossoms.

"My parents!" cried Loric, pulling Cymbril forward. She felt a happy relief at the kindness and love in their eyes. Laughing, Loric's parents swept him into their arms, and without even knowing who she was—or maybe they did know—they pulled Cymbril in, too.

In the tree limbs, a bird warbled on and on, fluttering from perch to perch. Cymbril couldn't hold back a giggle at the bird's wild excitement. "What is he singing about?"

"Oh, you know birds," Loric answered. "All sorts of things in a jumble, not finishing one thought before he starts another. Mostly, he's repeating 'The sun is coming up! The sun is coming up!'"

Rose-colored light grew in the east. Cymbril stood bathed in its glow, the darkness flowing away. The bird was right.

The Green Leaves of Eireigh

Frederic S. Durbin

Dorothy VanAndel Frisch

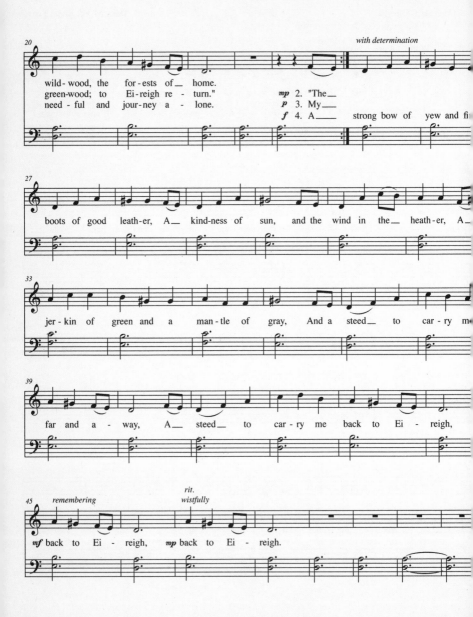

wild-wood, the for-ests of home.
green-wood; to Ei-reigh re - turn."
need - ful and jour-ney a - lone.

mp 2. "The
p 3. My
f 4. A strong bow of yew and fi

boots of good leath-er, A kind-ness of sun, and the wind in the heath-er, A

jer - kin of green and a man - tle of gray, And a steed to car - ry me

far and a - way, A steed to car - ry me back to Ei - reigh,

mf back to Ei - reigh, *mp* back to Ei - reigh.

Blue Were Her Eyes

Frederic S. Durbin

Dorothy VanAndel Frisch

With the motion of the sea and with a brogue (♩. = c. 60)

mf joyously

mf

1. Green were the lane and the leaves a-bove; Red were the ro-ses a-

round my love. Black was her hair, her skin like the dew; Her heart was a fire — that

mp

warmed — me through. Bright was the sky and gol-den the land, Soft was her breath as she

clasped my hand, And blue — as the o-cean, — blue — were her eyes. — *mf*

f grimly

2. Red were the ban-ners and crim-son the morn; To arms we rose at the long, loud horn.

5. Green were the lane and the leaves a-bove; Red were the ro-ses a-round my love.

White was her hair and cold the fire; Strong were her sons by an-oth-er sire.

Bright was the sky and gol-den the land, Sil-ver her tears as she

clasped my hand, And blue as the o-cean, blue were her eyes.

Blue as the o-cean, blue were her eyes.